BITCOIN HURRICANE

SIMCAVALIER ONE

Published in paperback in 2017 by Sixth Element Publishing
on behalf of Kate Baucherel

Sixth Element Publishing
Arthur Robinson House
13-14 The Green
Billingham TS23 1EU
Tel: 01642 360253
www.6epublishing.net

ISBN 978-1-912218-09-7

British Library Cataloguing in Publication Data. A catalogue record for this book is available from the British Library.

Printed in Great Britain.

BITCOIN HURRICANE

SIMCAVALIER ONE

KATE BAUCHEREL

Books by Kate Baucherel

The SimCavalier series

Bitcoin Hurricane (2017)

Hacked Future (2018)

Tangled Fortunes (2020)

Short stories in the Harvey Duckman Presents… series

Gridlock (Vol. 1, 2019)

White Christmas (Xmas Special, 2019)

Finch (Vol. 5, 2020)

Parrot Radio (Pirate Special, 2020)

Non-Fiction

Poles Apart: Challenges for business in the Digital Age
(MX Publishing, 2014)

Blockchain Hurricane: Origins, Applications
and Future of Blockchain and Cryptocurrency
(Business Expert Press, 2020)

CONTENTS

1: THE WORM

The worm crept through the virtual spaces of the world, threading itself imperceptibly through fibres and circuits, spreading silently across networks. It travelled patiently, carefully, a parasite replicating by laying eggs in host after host, spreading its presence exponentially around the globe. Its larvae would lie dormant for days, waiting for the opportunity to leap a new void, until the file in which the code slept was emailed to an unsuspecting recipient, and the journey continued.

Sometimes the worm landed in the lush breeding ground of a large institution, spreading across all the interconnected devices, taking advantage of gaps in outdated operating systems and in ancient software that unsuspecting users had clung to over the years. It slid unnoticed through ecosystems of unsecured smart devices, household appliances falling prey to the intruder thanks to manufacturers who cut corners and costs in the race to expand the Internet of Things. It crept into software companies, hitching a ride on downloads, and from there spread outwards like feathery seeds, riding on the wind of upgrades installed by trusting users.

At other times, it came up short, storming bastions protected by strong firewalls, passcodes, and the constant patrolling of the virtual ramparts by competent, conscientious cyber security troops; the worm kept probing for an opening, persisting in its attack until a slip, a trip, a minor human error, the simple click of an email, compromised even the best procedures and protocols.

A malicious little bundle of binary code, the worm was no empathetic artificial intelligence: it had no conscious sense of purpose, but was doing its job well. The surrogate offspring of a power in the shadows, carried to term by a scratch team of hungry developers commissioned on the Dark Web, it was born of greed and poverty. The only way out of the slums created by the fall of traditional industry, the devaluation of hard currency, the rising of the seas, the migration from extreme heat, and global economic upheaval was to embrace the digital world and code your way to freedom. The best underground developers commanded the highest fees; their employers played for the highest stakes.

Now, the worm was on the move. Its owners could not track its progress in its dormant state. They simply had to be patient, and make their plans around the predetermined moment of activation.

•

Sir Simon Winchester glowered at the wall of blank monitors for a moment, cursing under his breath, then turned to face his board members who had gathered hurriedly in the sumptuous and ancient oak-panelled room. In his decades of service to the bank, he had watched the fallout from wave upon wave of cyber attacks: the calls for robust systems, the horror at loss of data, the scramble of rivals to salvage their reputations as they went to the wall. As chief executive, one of his first and strongest commitments had been to reinforce and stabilise protection. Attacks never ceased: the bank simply had to be prepared.

"Current status, Bill?" he enquired levelly of the chief technology officer.

"Ransomware attack, activated twelve minutes ago," replied the CTO. "Pretty standard stuff, I think. We're still identifying the point of entry to our systems. There are global reports coming in over tech networks but nothing has gone public on the news channels yet."

"It helps that it's late in the day in the UK and Europe. That'll reduce the immediate impact," replied Sir Simon.

Bill nodded. "Good timing for us tonight, although it's starting to hit the States now. That'll cause a lot more trouble, and it's only Wednesday."

The bank's head of trading spoke up. "Cryptocurrency trading showed a spike in the minutes before the first reports came through, so there are some theories that it could be a targeted attack on the banking sector. Bill, what's your take on that?"

"Not sure. There is some reported fallout in other industries, but there's no clear indication of what weakness is being exploited yet."

Bill looked worried. He turned to Sir Simon. "This one's

spreading like wildfire internally, faster than we can close the gates. It's digging into some of the older software right at the heart of our operations. I need backup on this; we have our specialist team on standby."

Sir Simon nodded. They needed to react fast to neutralise the threat and get back to full operations. "Bring them in now, Bill. We need this virus closed down and cleaned out as fast as possible. Make the call."

Make the call? Bill winced at the anachronism, then nodded and pressed his thumb to a biometric scanner on his smartscreen. Accessing a private, uncompromised network, he sent a single word alert to a blockchain. A response dropped into the same block in seconds, completing the transaction and sealing the contract. The team was on the way.

Less than an hour later, two strangers were ushered into the boardroom. A young man in a grey hoodie stepped forwards and shook the hand of the CEO. "Good evening, Sir Simon. Ross White." He indicated his silent companion. "My colleague, Cameron Silvera."

Cameron stepped forward. "Sorry to hear about this disruption, sir. We'll tackle the security breach in due course; that's history. Our priority is to neutralise the threat. The team is setting up downstairs. We'll keep you in the loop."

Sir Simon nodded. "Anything you need, just ask."

•

An unassuming, middle-aged man sat alone at a round metal table outside a small coffee shop, slowly sipping an Americano. It was late morning. The pavements were quiet, and all the other tables at the café empty. The early rush of Thursday's commuters was over, and lunchtime was not far away. A shaft of weak sunlight glinted off the metal chairs under the café's awning.

His gaze fell on a harassed-looking woman, slightly overweight, her smart skirt straining at the waist and an ID badge dangling carelessly on a red lanyard, as she crossed the road towards the café and headed for the counter inside, pulling a smartscreen from her pocket.

"Gotcha!" exclaimed the observer as he fingered the scanning device tucked under his table. Any moment now, his mark would be firing up her network.

The latest cyber attack was causing havoc around the globe. There were rumours of a banking system crisis. Crypto transactions were running slow, with the more volatile digital currencies suspended altogether. The small network of legacy ATMs had been reporting problems dispensing old bank notes, which were still in use in some quarters where the digital world had not been fully embraced. Cyber security teams worldwide had been fighting to arrest the spread of the latest virus since it first hit the news last night. It looked like the attack had been slowed, but not in time for the businesses or the man in the street caught up in the mess. Shame for them, he thought, but this was the opportunity he'd been waiting for. They finally had a solid tip-off. They were going to find the man, this time. The next thing he needed in the hunt was an inside view, and the key was within reach.

Rushing into the café, the woman barely noticed another city worker grabbing a well-earned few minutes of peace on his break. All hell was breaking loose in the bank, and now she had to deal with an urgent message from the kids' school as well. Returning to work after a few years' break had seemed like a good idea at the time. So much had changed, and she was struggling to keep up. She ordered a skinny latte and a triple chocolate muffin, refuelling for the next few hours of her shift. The machine behind the counter whirred into action, and a roboserver selected her cake from a display and placed it on a waiting tray. Heading to a comfortable sofa and small wooden table in the corner, she thumbed her screen to life and scanned for a connection. Stretching to relieve aching muscles, she smiled tiredly at the friendly human waiter as her coffee and cake arrived. There was a discreet 'ping!' from her screen as the wifi connection opened. She logged back in to the work network and settled down to deal with her personal emails.

A discreet Bluetooth speaker chirruped in the watcher's ear. "She's picked up the connection… into the network… delivering the package now… okay, Andy, all clear."

Slipping the hidden device into his pocket, the man abandoned the dregs of his coffee and strolled nonchalantly away towards a waiting autocar.

•

Cameron groaned as the radio sparked into life. Woken from deep sleep in the darkness, disoriented, it took a few moments to come to. An activity sensor embedded in the still dark lightbulb automatically set the kettle on the other side of the wall to boil. Coffee was more essential to Cameron than light in the morning.

Hearing movement, a small black and white cat hopped up onto the bed and began kneading ecstatically, purring with the delight of a pet who knows its meal ticket has been roused and breakfast is not far away. Cameron stroked its head idly; the purring redoubled.

Snatches of news tumbled from the speakers in the wall by the bed, making no sense yet. It had been a tough thirty-six hours for Cameron, delivering payback in the form of sore eyes, dry mouth, and an aching back. The most recent cyber attack had caught yet another legacy system with its pants down, hidden deep and half-forgotten inside an apparently ultra-modern bank. Cameron's team had been working round the clock to limit the spread of infection. Who cared where it had come from – Asian tigers, Slavic trolls, the favelas of Rio de Janeiro, or bored high school dropouts – the ripples of disruption were slowing, thanks to a flash of classic Cameron intuition marking the first significant win of the battle, and the combined efforts of threat intelligence teams around the world to neutralise the virus. Snatching a few hours' sleep might have seemed to be an ill-afforded luxury, but it was a necessity. Tired teams made mistakes. Everyone had to be rested and ready to make leaps of logic in containing, defusing, and mopping up after the threat.

The sounds from the radio gradually formed themselves into words. "I come to pick up my money and they said I can't, there's been a cyber attack. I don't know what one of them even is," complained a strident voice. "Why isn't it working? Why don't they do something?"

Cameron flung back the covers in disgust, eliciting a mutter of protest from a slumbering form, and a startled squeak from the cat, dislodged from its cosy nest. Cameron was already half way to the kitchen as the kettle steamed.

Cameron reached into the cupboard to select a clean bowl, grabbed the nearest box of cereal, and turned to the tiny but serviceable refrigerator to find some milk. Despite embracing all things digital and working in tech, Cameron held the very clear opinion that while a smart kettle might be utterly essential in the provision of timely coffee, a smart fridge was just a ridiculous concept. Sniffing suspiciously at the carton, the milk passed the test. Cameron splashed it over the cereal and part of the table, cursed, and reached for a cloth.

The cat circled its food bowl, mewing as if it was half starved. Cameron had no idea if it had been fed two days or two hours ago. No matter: an extra meal wouldn't bother a cat the way it might bother a human who constantly monitored calorie intake, weight gain, daily steps, and heart attack risk factors, in an effort to keep medical costs to a minimum.

Munching on cereal, Cameron glanced at a discreet cylinder tucked on the shelf. "Can you read out my emails?"

"I'm sorry, I didn't understand that. Did you want to read about snails?" replied a smooth voice.

Cameron swallowed. "Read out my emails."

The 'bot paused. "You have one hundred and thirty-six unread messages. You have seventy-eight automated mailings. You have three priority messages from Ross White, four messages from Charlie Silvera, two messages from..."

"Delete the automated messages," snapped Cameron. "Volume down, and play the priority emails." Another spoonful of cereal, another swig of coffee, and the latest updates from the past few hours unfolded.

"Hi Cameron," came Ross's voice. "Enjoy your rest? We've been working our butts off here. We've pretty much dealt with the surface disruption, but the older stuff in this bloody banking system is wide open and needs patching. There are still a few reports of compromised servers in the wider world but the decrypt you developed is fixing those. The antidote that's circulating seems to have stopped virus transmission dead in its tracks." Ross sounded almost cheerful. "Now we're trying to settle the currency systems. We've had to close down all the ATMs country-wide for a short while, so there will be hell on when the public gets wind of this. Cryptocurrency trading is all suspended. We may be looking at a soft fork to upgrade protection, which will take days to organise, and that could get ugly if someone decides to dig their heels in. I'm knackered and I need to get some fresh air. See you when you get back."

"Hi Cameron, me again. The guys want some breakfast. Can you grab a few things on the way in?"

"Cameron, we've picked up a really odd subroutine embedded in this virus. Nothing I've seen before. I need you to take a look. See you shortly."

•

Mystified, Cameron dropped the cereal bowl in the sink, and crept quietly into the bedroom to fetch some clothes: clean underwear, jeans, casual sports shoes, t-shirt, and a respectable long-sleeved top. Spring weather in England could be unpredictable from hour to hour; best to be prepared for all eventualities. 'Cast ne'er a clout till May be out' had been one of their grandmother's favourite sayings, trotted out every time either Cameron or Charlie dared to leave the house without a jumper. Cameron smiled at the memory of the tiny, rotund woman who had baked the most exquisite cakes for her treasured grandchildren, terrified her own offspring, and ruled the whole family with an iron will. The saying was becoming redundant these days; climate change had eliminated the spring frosts, although the rain still fell, and the nights could be cool.

Closing the apartment door carefully, Cameron bounded down the three flights of stairs with the renewed energy of someone with a mystery to solve, greeting neighbours as they too headed out for work. A familiar gaggle of young people, they were not exactly friends, but nodding acquaintances, occasional drinking partners, fellow fitness enthusiasts, part of the landscape. They knew very little about each other's lives or backgrounds, and co-existed in those happy, prosperous golden years between the intense undergraduate rite of passage at university, and settling down to family life in the suburbs.

"Hey Cameron," called Jasvinder as they met on the second-floor landing, "How's it going? Didn't see you at training last night – out for a works do, were you?"

"Something like that," grinned Cameron. "Long day and a hot date." Jasvinder had no idea what Cameron actually did for a living – some sort of robotics training thing, wasn't it? – and it was best to keep it that way. Fighting cyber crime seemed so exotic but there were dangers to being identified. Modern-day spies, Charlie had once dubbed the team. As soon as an identity got out there, it was retirement– or worse.

They streamed out of the revolving main doors of the small apartment block into fresh air and early morning sunshine. A haze of blossom had appeared on the cherry trees lining the pavement. One of the guys yawned, and sneezed violently.

"Dammit, forgot to get hayfever meds. Starting so early this year." He set off in the direction of the nearby underground station.

Cameron started to follow then hesitated, deciding to

walk instead. Traffic was busy, the underground would be heaving, and it would probably be quicker on foot. Could do with some extra steps in the fitness log, too, after a day and half of sitting at a screen in the depths of the bank. The bright weather was unlikely to last in any case: better make the most of it.

With four lanes of traffic crawling silently down the main road, and deep in thought, Cameron was unaware of a car pulling out from the side street in pursuit of its quarry. The route north to the river was automatic and familiar. Turning onto the High Street, Cameron walked briskly past brightly painted shop fronts, ducking instinctively as a delivery drone flew down and through the archway of an ancient coaching inn that had once welcomed horse-drawn carriages bound for the south. The smell of warm bread broke the reverie. Diving into the bakery in a small row of shops, Cameron quickly selected the team's favourite pastries from a tempting display. The owner bagged them up, spots of buttery translucence appearing on the paper, a rich scent rising from the bag.

Cameron followed the main road towards the river, avoiding the busy market today, and passing under the shadow of the Shard, its gleaming mirrored flanks reflecting the distorted images of a mass of drones rising from the market on their way to deliver fresh food across the city, and its pointed tip breaking the wispy clouds high above. A fresh breeze rustled the paper bag as Cameron crossed the Thames, Tower Bridge standing proud to the east. A river ferry hooted as it passed under the bridge on its way to the pier. The tide was out, exposing mudflats and beaching small boats. The smell that wafted up on the breeze was musty but not unpleasant; pollution in the river had improved immeasurably since Cameron was a child. Entering the busy City district, Cameron disappeared into the crowds that bustled through the maze of bleached white stone buildings, heading for the bank.

•

The two men went unnoticed as they sat in their autocar in a side street, drinking endless cardboard cups of coffee, and watching the apartment door revolve as it disgorged its chattering residents in all directions. Few families; these were mainly young professionals able to pay the price of living close to the action in the capital. Property prices were notoriously high this close to the river, and across London as a whole. The old north-south divide had been repaired when Parliament sat for a few years in the wilderness of Northern England during refurbishments to the Palace of Westminster, although with the return to the bright lights of London some of the old competitiveness between regions had resurfaced. Now, the economic battle was drawn along digital lines: the haves, with their smartscreens and fibre connections and biometrics; the have nots, relying on paper forms and paper money, resistant to the digital skills that pave the pathway from poverty to success.

A short blonde girl in high heels and bright colours emerged, chatting to a young black guy with a phone in his hand and a sweater slung over his arm. A tall, unconsciously elegant, dark-haired woman, dressed down in jeans with a smart leather backpack, blinking as she stepped into the sunlight. A slim Asian lad in a smart suit and blue turban who headed straight for the small car park. A pale young man, muscled and fit, scowling at the world, casual in a grey hoodie, stumbled out through the door.

"I don't believe it, that's our boy," exclaimed Giles, dropping his empty cup behind the seat and grabbing his camera.

"Are you sure?" asked his companion.

Giles sighed. "Matches the most likely person on the CCTV images from the bank. Right place. I'm guessing he hasn't slept much for the past couple of days, and this guy certainly looks pretty tired. You'll need to direct. Switch off the autonav."

Traffic was heavy and slow on the main road. Giles had no problem snapping image after image as his companion teased the car along. The young man approached a row of shops, and disappeared momentarily from view. The autocar stopped at a set of traffic lights long enough for Giles to see him emerge carrying a bag, before the one-way system swept all the traffic away to the east, and they could see him no more.

"Get any good ones?"

"Think so," replied Giles. "Clearer than the CCTV,

anyway. Hardly the Laughing Cavalier, is he? Who'd have thought he's the brains behind saving the world?"

2: SIMCAVALIER

Thirty six hours earlier.

Ross was the first to arrive at the bank after the alert came in. Young, fit and athletic, his favourite grey hoodie always gave his pale features a drawn look. He loped into the bank's sumptuous marble hallway, dark wood staircases sweeping away to upper floors, and chandeliers sparkling in the late afternoon light.

Approaching the long reception desk under the gaze of its CCTV cameras, he gave a code word to the smart receptionist and was swiftly issued with his security pass. A PA hurried down the broad staircase, his brogues silent on the thick pile of the carpet, and ushered Ross through the barriers and up to a small, empty meeting room.

Ross paced around the room, ignoring the six high-backed wooden chairs set neatly around a polished table. He paused to gaze down from the tall window to the street below. The pavements were less crowded than before, and the odd streetlight flicked into life as the sun dipped down below the rooftops. He spotted several familiar figures approaching the bank from different directions, called away from family and friends, work and play, to go into battle.

Cameron appeared at the door fifteen minutes later. "Team's all here, Ross. Ready to roll."

The PA reappeared and guided them up another floor to the boardroom. Oak panels spoke of the bank's history, a wall of monitors of its future, and a sense of controlled concern emanating from the gathered men and women spoke of its immediate present. Ross glanced at Cameron, then stepped forward and shook the hand of the bank's chief executive. They were underway.

•

Bill the CTO showed Ross and Cameron down to the heart of the building.

"We've set your team up in the main operations room." He gestured to an open door. "Coffee, water, snacks in this kitchen, breakout space for you too. Bathrooms are just down the hall, I'll get some towels and freshen up packs into the showers. You have full access to everything in this section using your passes. There are security personnel in reception and I'll stick around for as long as you need me."

Cameron smiled. "Many thanks, Bill, appreciate it. We'll get started straight away, need to stop the beastie spreading before we do anything else. I'll want your help when we zip the systems back up and patch the holes, but right now I think you can leave us to it."

Bill nodded. "I think you have all the access codes you need. Call me at any time if you need something. Here's my number." He headed wearily for the stairs, as Cameron and Ross entered the operations room.

Six pairs of eyes turned towards them.

"All set, boss," said a short, chubby man in jeans and a garish rock band t-shirt, nodding at Cameron.

"Thanks Sandeep." Cameron paused. "Okay. Joel, see if you can get hold of a clean copy of this virus. Check the tech communities, dig into that last NSA dump on the Dark Web, there has to be a copy circulating somewhere. You and I can work on rebutting the attack externally. Ross, you, Pete and Ella get into the bank system and quarantine that critter. Close it down, stop it spreading further through the network than it already has. Noor, I want you to keep track of other compromised systems and open communications with the teams working on them. Sandeep, you and Susie work with Noor, and have a look at possible breaches too. See if there are any systematic failures or if it's just an ID 10-T error." Cameron grinned. "I love a challenge. Let's go."

•

Andy was tired. He ran a hand through his untidy brown hair, sighed, and leaned his elbows on the desk, thinking. His editor was getting impatient. After three years of chasing whispers and mirages, he still had to produce the cyber security scoop he'd promised. He was a good tech journalist, but one story kept eluding him. Who were the people behind the fight against cyber crime? He felt like the frustrated hacks in the superhero films his dad had loved, trying to unmask a hero, while the alter ego hid in plain sight.

Right now, though, there was a more urgent story to cover. There were ripples on the forums, a sudden upsurge of activity, distant whispers of a new cyber attack. Andy took a slug of coffee and shook his head, refocusing. He scoured his network, seeking confirmation and clarity before writing his piece for the hungry rolling news that broadcast all day, every day. As he searched, a notification appeared in the corner of his screen. An anonymous message, which immediately grabbed his attention.

"The SimCavalier rides into battle. This one's spreading like the Great Fire."

His heart was racing. This was unprecedented. He'd been following this shadowy figure through several years of high profile cyber security alerts. The name appeared on tech forums, quoted in awed discussions among the top echelons of the threat intelligence community. This – person? entity? group? – seemed to be at the forefront of combating the increasingly steady waves of cyber crime, hacking, and ransomware. Disrupted by the failure of traditional encryption less than a decade ago, the world was still struggling to manage digital security. Andy's painstaking research showed clearly that without the diligent and inspired work of the SimCavalier, it might have descended further into anarchy. He was a true modern hero, and should be celebrated. Andy couldn't understand why he sought to stay in the shadows.

It looked as if years of gradual infiltration into the

cyber security community had finally paid off. Someone was on Andy's side, ready to help.

"Call Giles," he barked at the portal.

A moment later the voice call connected. "What's up, boss?"

"You've picked up this latest cyber attack, yes?"

"Sure. Kicked off around an hour, hour and a half ago by all accounts. Most reports coming from the United States, but I guess that's because they've been hit in the middle of the day. A few from Europe. Getting ready to break it on the news channels."

"It's here. There's a case right here in London. And he's on it."

"Wow. Shit. Sorry. I mean, how do you know? There are no confirmed reports of infection here in the UK yet."

"We've just had a tipoff. 'The SimCavalier rides into battle.' Can't get much clearer than that. The guy is mobilising against the latest threat. And as for location, this says 'spreading like the Great Fire'. Great Fire of London? Nothing else it can be."

Giles was sceptical. "That's incredible. But where do we take it from here? London's a bloody big place. He'll have it killed in short order and be gone before we get close to him."

Andy laughed. "I think it's a bit easier than that. Where's the Monument to the Great Fire of London? It's smack in the middle of the City. I reckon we're looking at a bank."

•

Cameron laughed as the ransom demand appeared on Ross's monitor. A dancing cocktail gif dominated the screen with a flashing neon message: 'Welcome to the Speakeasy. Bitcoin Accepted Here'. "Hah, brilliant. At least the bastards have a sense of humour."

"Doesn't make it any easier to crack," grumbled Ross. He was aching after a day's hard training, and regretted missing out on a recuperative massage and a relaxing evening. "Fairly standard stuff, though. Do we know what it looks like in the wild?"

Joel shook his head, dreadlocks swaying. "Nothing yet. Plenty of reports coming through but we don't have a dump of the code. Watching the usual channels."

Noor piped up from her desk. "I'm in touch with a team in New York, and another in Sydney. They're seeing a lot of hits in the financial sector."

Cameron thought for moment. "Interesting, Noor, stay on top of that. Ella, can you run some models on trading over the past week. It could be just coincidence that this is the first wave of reports, but we'd better eliminate all possibilities."

"Right you are." Ella slipped on her headphones and opened a secure, anonymous browser. Her hands glided across the screen as she captured data from pools across the world and began the painstaking process of analysis.

Ross settled into his seat. "Okay, Pete, let's roll. What's tonight's playlist? Better pick something to keep us awake."

Pete scrolled through the options. "You said it. Melissa

Mix?" Solid bass lines and fast rhythms kicked into life, quickly muffled as the two of them pulled their headsets on and got to work.

Cameron turned to Sandeep and Susie. "Okay Susie, in at the deep end. Your first big job. How are you feeling?"

Susie smiled nervously. "I'll be fine. It'll be interesting to see where the breach was. I thought this place was as tight as a drum. I guess I was wrong."

"The bigger they are, the harder they fall. There's always a way in. Sandeep will keep you straight. Can you both make sure you do a wide sweep for all potential gaps and compromises? We need to leave this place sewn up properly. There'll be other penetrations no one knows about."

Sandeep and Susie nodded. Cameron turned back to Joel. "Anything yet?"

"Still digging. I'm keeping an eye on that Bitcoin wallet, too. There've been a handful of ransom payments already. You'd think people would learn there's no point paying."

Cameron sighed. "Me too. If no one paid there'd be no point writing viruses and we'd have a quiet life. I had plans this evening." Joel raised a questioning eyebrow; Cameron refused to be drawn. "I'd better make my excuses. I don't mind, really. This is too interesting. I do love my job."

Joel laughed. "You're quite the hero, Cameron. I'm happy, I got out of rugby training tonight; I won't be so sore now when we play on Saturday. It's coming up to the end of the season, anyway, so it'll soon be time for a proper rest." He turned back to the scrolling screen.

"Aha! We've got our first look. Here we go, Speakeasy code dump. Nice work. Let's see what this one's made of."

•

Midnight chimes rang out across London, from the rolling boom of Big Ben to the distinctive sounds of the ancient towers of the city. The bells of St Clements, Shoreditch and Old Bailey sang out their tunes, passed down the generations in the old nursery rhyme for three hundred years. Deep in the bank, the bells went unheard; the team was taking a well-earned break.

"Land it on the top," squealed Ella, as Pete expertly guided a small drone around the room and up towards a hanging light fitting.

Susie was doubled up with laughter. "I can't believe you guys."

The little drone, a toy modelled on a spaceship from the latest Hollywood blockbuster, dropped down on the light and a ragged round of applause rang out.

Pete swore. "I can't get it to lift off again – that light's blocking the signal. Hold on." He moved his chair to the wall, clambered up and stretched high on tiptoe to achieve the right angle. Pete rocked precariously on his perch, and the drone wobbled and swooped off the light. Ella ducked as it went overhead.

"Pizza in the kitchen," called Ross. Pete jumped off his chair and parked the drone as they all trooped out, inviting smells wafting from the corridor. Greasy cardboard boxes were open on the table, and the hungry team members grabbed a couple of slices each. Ross sat apart, munching on chicken and salad, making at least some effort to stick to the nutrition required of his punishing training regime.

Cameron sat at the head of the table, devouring a slice piled high with meat and chillies. "Good work so far, guys. Let's take stock. Ross, over to you. How far have you got?"

"We've started to dismantle the cage. I'll need you to get your head around a decrypt over the next few hours. The ransom is masking a couple of subroutines. It's like a bloody Russian Doll, every time we dig deeper we come across another element. It's not particularly complex but it's taking time. Most of the systems are untouched, particularly the newer, more transparent software. Blockchains are okay. It's the older stuff where we're finding weaknesses."

"Hmm. We need to have a chat with Bill about legacy systems. That can wait until the morning, though. Sandeep?"

Sandeep, lounging on a bright orange beanbag, glanced at Susie. "Nothing so far, boss. The security protocols are pretty tight, which is what we expected. We're combing through mail servers and reverse engineering from Ross's work. We'll find it."

Noor looked up. "Go back in time. A couple of folks I'm chatting to who've found their breaches have mentioned a long lag between penetration and execution, anything up to eight weeks so far. We'd expect that in a phishing attack, compromising the network then gradually digging deep over time, but this looks and acts like a simple worm."

The group fell silent, reflecting. Cameron absent-mindedly reached for another slice of pizza. "Anyone else?"

The others stepped up the table and refilled their plates.

"The thing I don't understand," continued Cameron after a pause, "is that this looks like ransomware, and it's certainly collecting a bit of dosh, but it's not making them rich, and it has these extra bells and whistles attached. Why? What's going on?"

Ross shrugged, left the table, and flopped onto an empty beanbag. "Dunno. Don't care right now. I'm tired. Let's get it nailed and then you can worry about motives."

Ella looked up at Cameron. "I may have an idea. I think I'm getting somewhere with the financial modelling. It's hard to spot, but I've confirmed what the bank indicated. There's a spike in cryptocurrency futures trading just before the attack."

Cameron's eyes widened. The others looked confused.

"So?" asked Sandeep.

Ella turned to him, looking serious. "Okay, so people who buy and sell stocks, shares, money, they hope that if they can buy something now, then the price will go up so they can sell it and make a profit. Yeah?"

Sandeep nodded. "Sure, that makes sense."

Ella continued. "So, futures work a bit differently.

People make money when the price goes down. They say, I'll short sell that thing, I don't know, like a thousand of those shares for twenty coins each. So, the trader 'lends' them a thousand shares to sell, and they get twenty thousand coins in their wallet from the buyer. A bit later on, they have to buy a thousand shares to give back to the trader – do you follow? So, if the shares are still worth twenty coins, they've broken even, if it's gone up they've lost money. If the price has dropped, though, it might only cost ten coins a share to re-buy, so boom! Profit of ten thousand coins."

Sandeep blinked. "That's pretty fucked up. This really happens?"

"Sure," replied Ella. "Common practice, been around for centuries, literally. It was all stocks and shares and hard currency back then, obviously, but people have been shorting cryptocurrency for thirty years, especially in the early days when Bitcoin first took off and the price was bouncing up and down. Lots of winners, lots of losers. Fun times."

Ross frowned. "Are you saying there could be some connection?"

"Not sure," replied Ella. "It's a tiny spike, could be a coincidence, but if I'd given up on making money from ransoms, I'd look at other options."

Cameron looked at the clock. "We need to get back to work. Ella, can you develop those models. See what you can find in terms of location and timing of trades, any trackback to the parties involved, and if there've been any unusual profits taken. It'll be interesting to see how that pans out. You may be onto something."

Standing up and stretching, Cameron stacked the empty pizza boxes, while Joel collected the plates and dropped them into the dishwasher. The team returned to their desks, headphones back on, concentration restored.

Cameron's fingers flexed and dived onto the keyboard with renewed energy, seeking a route to decryption, and an antidote to stop the virus spreading.

•

Bill arrived at the bank just before 8am and headed downstairs. All was quiet. Poking his head around the door of the breakout room, he saw a pile of pizza boxes on the table and three figures sprawled, asleep, on the beanbags. The sound of running water betrayed a fourth person taking a shower.

Opening the door to the operations room, Bill found Cameron, Ross, Susie and Noor deep in conversation. The animated discussion broke off as soon as they saw Bill arrive.

"Morning all. No midnight calls so I guess you're making progress?" Bill sounded hopeful. "The Board meets at nine. What can I tell them? Are you coming up to brief them?"

Cameron stood up. "Come and have a look at this, Bill. See what we've been up to. Ross, Susie, can you sort out some breakfast for the troops?"

As Ross and Susie closed the door behind them, Noor returned to her desk, watching the flurry of new forum posts as IT staff across the country arrived at work and discovered new instances of the infection. They were logging into the threat intelligence forums, comparing notes, seeking fixes. Cameron took Bill across to a bank of monitors.

"Internal stuff first. Here's the first thing every infected user sees…" The dancing cocktails appeared on the screen. "It's been dubbed the Speakeasy virus, for obvious reasons. Now, that's a mask using old encryption technology, and the data behind it is still sound. I know we don't encrypt for high security these days, it's too easy for hackers to crack, but it still foxes the man in the street, which is why ransomware trojans haven't stopped doing the rounds. It's taken us most of the night to develop the decrypt for this bit, but it's done. We were the first to release that part of the solution worldwide, I'm well chuffed. Great team effort."

Bill smiled at the pride in Cameron's voice. "So, we're up and running again?"

"No, still a fair way to go for you, I'm afraid. This encryption was hiding a couple of subroutines, bits of hidden code. They don't affect the newer systems but they've got their suckers into an SQL database with dodgy security. First question, Bill, what the hell is something that archaic doing down there in your bank servers?"

Shamefaced, Bill explained. "We inherited a mess. After

Brexit when the Euro traders moved out, the City had to innovate, and they went deep into cryptocurrency to survive. We needed to keep the original systems running for hard currencies, at least until consumers caught up, and some of those dated back even further, pre-2000. Investment was all channelled into cryptocurrency trading and the old systems were left behind. Eventually, support ran out, no new security updates. Thirty years on, enough customers still insist on using hard currencies that we have to maintain the service. All the effort we've put in to get them up to speed on digital and they treat bank notes like a bloody comfort blanket. We never thought we'd still be running these systems now."

Cameron felt sorry for him. The work the bank had done to secure their old network against generic attack was pretty good, truth be told. Another patch would do the trick – until the next cyber criminal innovation.

"Do you know where it got in?" he asked.

"Closing in on it," replied Cameron. "We know it's an email penetration, just have to identify the exact route. For now, we're concentrating on sorting those hidden subroutines, and identifying an antidote to halt the spread of the virus. It's no use decrypting when it'll just re-infect. I think we're pretty close."

Bill nodded. "Okay. I'll advise the Board that we're offline today but we're getting close to complete repair. Good job. I'll leave you to it." He turned to the door as

Ella walked in, coffee and muffin in hand, hair tousled and damp. "Looks like breakfast's arrived."

"Bye, Bill, see you later. We'll keep you posted."

•

The train glided silently up to the platform, wheels clicking on the rails. Swept through the doors in a crowd of commuters, Andy found a seat and pulled out his smartscreen. He checked the news channels for the latest public announcements about the ongoing cyber attack. It had a name: Speakeasy. Businesses around the world were reporting compromised networks. Advice was being repeated to sit tight, pay no ransom, wait for the tech guys to work their magic. All very bland.

He needed the inside dish. Logging on to a threat intelligence community under a long-held assumed identity, it was immediately evident that the decrypt had been developed, verified, and was rippling out to the world. He dipped in and out of discussions, dropping the odd comment to maintain his cover: 'High five, guys.' 'Looks sound to me.' 'Great work! Deploying now, I'll let you know how it goes.' Weaving through the threads, he was looking for one handle in particular – and there it was. 6.20am UK time. Post author: @SimCavalier. 'Tested and running, Speakeasy decrypt process and batch file attached.' A string of virtual applause from hundreds of forum members, and several verifications of the fix, showed up as replied to the simple post.

Andy sat back, satisfied, as the train dived into the tunnels beneath North London and slowed as it approached its destination.

The net was closing.

Andy's surveillance guy was waiting for him in a meeting room just off the bustling office floor. A small coffee machine in the corner sparked into life as it detected Andy's arrival, delivering exactly the right dose of caffeine to match his recorded sleep patterns from the previous night. This morning, it was one strong cup.

"Hi, Andy, good run in this morning?"

Andy took a swig of coffee and winced. "Very smooth, thanks – not the coffee, the commute. Long night though."

"Saw the news. I guess your boy is in the middle of it all?"

"Oh yes. We're as close as we've ever been to this guy and we have the next piece of the puzzle. Our tipoff indicates that he's operating somewhere in the City of London. It's still a big place, and we can't cover the whole lot, especially as we still can't identify him by sight. Stroke of luck, though: it looks like he's first to figure out the decrypt, as usual, and we've got the original post on this forum."

The monitor on the wall glowed as Andy brought up the discussion thread for his colleague to see.

"Can we pinpoint where that was sent from? There's a good chance he was still on site."

The surveillance expert nodded. "We can dig around in

the background of the forum. The IP addresses for each post are in there somewhere. It's a private community sitting on generic software, and the admins will have access for moderation and management. Shouldn't be too hard to crack."

"Get onto it," said Andy. "As soon as we know where he is, we'll have a chance to get a good look at him, at last."

•

It was late morning when the final strike of the battle was delivered. Noor turned excitedly to the rest of the team. "We did it! Cameron, it's stopped. No new reports. The antidote is holding."

A ragged cheer went up from the exhausted group. Cameron lounged back in the soft leather chair – only the finest furniture, even here in the depths of the bank – and smiled broadly. "Brilliant work guys. Just fantastic."

Ross stood up and stretched. "Looking good here, too. Not spread any further in the network. System is still compromised, but we've contained the subroutines in those deep databases. One's executed, but the other's dormant for now. Odd. Anyway, next step, kill the activated code and clean up."

"No," countered Cameron. "Next step, you go and get some rest. Ross, Susie, Noor, Ella, Pete, get your heads down. We'll probably need you back here, not before early evening, though. Joel, Sandeep, let's grab some lunch and then we'll make a start on the subroutines. We'll stay in close touch with external teams, make sure we really have neutralised it out there, and share anything we crack here."

Ross nodded gratefully and shuffled to the door, exhausted. He'd had no time to recover from the previous day's training session and he was stiff and aching all over. He didn't expect to find it hard to sleep today, regardless of the bright spring sunshine that would be illuminating his bedroom. "Goodnight, folks. See you later."

The other four followed him out, eager to get some rest.

Cameron turned to the remaining two team members. "Sorry guys, I know you're tired too, at least you managed a snooze through the night. We'll go steady this afternoon and we'll all be in our beds before we know it. Right. Lunch. Let's get out of here."

The coffee shop opposite the bank was full to bursting; it was the busiest time of the day. The crowd swept the three of them, unresisting, along the wide pavement towards a pedestrian area full of small boutiques, cafes and restaurants. The spring day was still cool in the shade of the surrounding buildings, so there were plenty of spaces at outdoor tables. Cameron, Joel and Sandeep flopped onto vacant chairs in the fresh air, relieved to be outside.

•

Andy leaned over to look closer at the monitor. The CCTV images were grainy, following the to-ing and fro-ing of several hundred people as they passed through the bank's reception. "Have you picked any likely leads up yet?"

The surveillance man nodded. "We have a live feed right now, which isn't telling us much, but we've been able to access the archives for the last twenty-four hours. They're much more interesting. Look here." He scrolled back and froze the frame. "Okay. Your tipoff came in at 6.15pm. About twenty minutes before this, there's a flurry of activity. Some big suits have arrived, straight through security. The rest of the traffic is going the other way." He tapped the screen. "Now, look, I think this is our man. Arrives on his own, against the flow, barely waits, they're obviously expecting him. About ten minutes later we see a couple more coming in. There's a hiccup in the recording, you can only just see them arriving and we can't tell how many are in the group, or where they went."

Andy nodded. "Got anything else?"

"Yep." He fast forwarded, and pointed at the screen. "We spotted him again, with a girl, we think, leaving the building just after eight this morning. Fifteen minutes later, and here they both are coming back in. Loads of bags. Breakfast for the troops? I think they've been in there all night."

"That fits," said Andy. "The communities we've been tracking have a bunch of comments overnight from our boy, and he released that Speakeasy decrypt early this morning. Is he still there?"

"No. Here, this is some of the first live footage we accessed. There's our guy in the hoodie, four others with him, walking out with the rest of the bank staff for an early lunch. I'm still watching, but he hasn't come back. Missed him again, huh?"

Andy slammed his hand on the desk in irritation. "It's got to be him. Okay, if nothing else, we know what he looks like. That's a big step forward. Keep an eye on any more movement. If he comes back in, I want to know."

A thought struck him. "He has to sleep sometime. He's got to have a home. Can you get back into that forum, identify @SimCavalier posts for say the last three months, pick out any residential locations? He arrived pretty fast last night, so he's based in London somewhere. If we can place this guy in the hoodie at the right location, we've got our man."

3: A WARNING

Charlie closed the heavy front door behind him with a sigh of relief. Mornings were never peaceful in the Silvera household, with three kids getting ready for school and a bouncy Labradoodle anticipating a long walk. The sound of Sameena directing the children from the breakfast table, to the bathroom, and to find their bags and shoes, faded as he strode across the gravel to the car. He'd lost track of whether they needed guitars, violins, swimming kit, or all three on Thursdays; hopefully his wife had the timetable in hand. Right now, his focus was on the business, on the cusp of completing a major car components order. Pulling out of their drive and up the leafy lane out of the village, he set the route to the factory, and flicked on the news channel.

"…said the Prime Minister. Returning to our main story: organisations across the globe are battling an ongoing cyber attack, dubbed the Speakeasy Virus. The majority of incidents have been reported in the banking sector, with disruption to currency trading, although the attack has not been confined to financial institutions. Several established global businesses have announced network failures, and small companies are equally badly hit. The authorities are advising those affected not to pay any ransom demand. Over now to our correspondent in the City of London."

"Initial reports of this attack came in yesterday evening, just after 6pm UK time," announced a reporter. "Threat intelligence professionals across the world have been battling to crack the codes throughout the night, but the first major breakthrough came here, in central London, with the development of a decryption programme by an as yet unknown British specialist. There are continued reports of infection, but it would appear the threat is diminishing. Now, back to the studio."

Charlie sighed. He suspected Cameron was right in the middle of it all, and would be pretty busy mopping up the mess. Hopefully it would all be over by the weekend; Cameron was due to visit, to celebrate Sameena's birthday.

"Incoming call," announced the car.

"Answer," said Charlie, gazing out at the familiar passing scenery.

"Morning Charlie," came the voice of his second in command. "Are you on your way in? We've had a bit of problem."

Charlie's heart sank. "What's up, Holly?"

There was a pause, and Charlie heard Holly calling indistinctly to someone else in the office. "Sorry Charlie, just sorting out Production. The network went down at our host around 3am. Looks like they got caught by this latest cyber attack on one of their shared servers. The remote backups should have kicked in by now, but they're holding off to check that the ransomware hasn't spread to connected facilities."

Charlie's good mood evaporated. "What's happening in the factory, Holly? We shouldn't be affected. There arc all sorts of service agreements in place."

Holly sounded annoyed. "All we're getting is blank screens, and the printers are on standby. As far as we know our dedicated servers are okay, and we understand the host company has gotten hold of the decryption software now, but all comms have been shut down as a precaution. Not a lot we can do, but wanted to let you know before you walk into a silent building."

"Okay. Thanks. Forewarned is forearmed, huh. See what you can find out about expected restore time. I'll see you shortly." Great start to the day, thought Charlie, as the call terminated. The company was hot on minimising human failures in cyber security – they'd had Cameron's team in to do the training, of course – but having an external breach affect the host of their supposedly secure cloud was another matter. The hosting company must be beside themselves, their previously spotless reputation on the line. How had this snuck through their defences?

Whatever malicious code had compromised the cloud wasn't Charlie's greatest problem right now. They needed the printers back online in the factory; those components had to be out on deadline, and they were already skating close to contract penalties for going over time.

"Call Matt at Owens and York." The voice call connected. "Morning Matt, sorry to bother you. Bit of a hiccup – we're on standby in the factory, waiting for our host to decrypt their servers. We're okay, but there's been a breach somewhere up the line and all our systems are dormant as a precaution. Can you check the cyber attack clauses in this contract and drop a marker into the blockchain? Just need to cover ourselves in case the delay takes us into penalties."

"Sure, Charlie, I'll get onto that now." The lawyers were good at their job.

Sometimes Charlie yearned for the factory floor he recalled as a youngster, fresh out of university and learning the ropes in the family firm. He'd been so keen to jump on the emerging technology bandwagon back in 2025, and it was true that his enthusiasm for change and shrewd application of the right solutions had sealed the future of the business where less agile competitors had gone to the wall. Right now, though, he'd trade the expanse of 3D printers nurtured by his modern workforce for the skilled machine tooling teams that had retired years before.

The car paused at the junction and turned on to the dual carriageway, stopping and starting in the queue of autocars that crawled towards the town. Charlie sighed and leaned back in his seat. "I never could get the hang of Thursdays," he muttered to himself, with an ironic half-smile.

A message pinged: eleven year old Nina's face appeared on the monitor. "Dad, don't forget to pick me up from netball tonight. See you later. Bye." Charlie knew one of the advantages of living so close to work was the luxury of seeing his kids grow up, picking them up from school, being part of their daily lives. Tonight, though, Nina would have to rely on her mother.

•

Refreshed, Cameron, Sandeep and Joel got back to work. Light streamed in to the basement through skylights from ground level, illuminating dust motes in the air.

"Sandeep, on the comms please, see how that decrypt is going down and check that the spread of the virus has really stopped. Joel, let's dig into these subroutines."

Picking a path through the archaic operating systems, Cameron stalked the first subroutine as it whirled around the database. Once identified, it was a simple matter to isolate the code and pull it out onto a separate quarantined machine. Bringing the code up onto the monitor, Joel and Cameron ran through each line. It was tiny, repetitive thing, programmed to pick up data and move it around, scrambling the database, wiping any meaning from the information that had been stored there.

Cameron pointed to a short line of code. "See here, it's searching for a file. I thought that was a data dump, but check this later instruction. If it finds it, the routine terminates."

"Ah, you genius," breathed Joel. "Let's give it what it wants, shall we?" He turned to the main interface and navigated to the right directory. "No, nothing there. Here goes." Quickly and efficiently, he created a new file and dropped it in. The two of them watched the activity of the SQL database on a separate monitor. Moments later, the queries stopped.

Cameron and Joel high fived each other. Sandeep looked up, grinning.

"Let's get that out to the web," said Cameron. "Anyone else picked it up yet?"

Sandeep laughed. "Sorry boss, the guys on the East Coast beat you to it by a few minutes. I'll drop a confirmation of the fix to them. I guess it's only a temporary thing?"

Cameron nodded. "We'll make sure it's in the full patch when we restore the databases from backup. The operating system down there is so old there'll be nothing coming out from the big tech companies, I guess. We'll need to be prepared for more of the same now this is vulnerability is out in the open. At least we'll know the first place to look, another time."

Joel looked up at the skylights. Daylight was fading. "That took longer than I thought. It's already five o'clock. Shall we take a break?" He looked at Cameron, who nodded in agreement.

"The databases look stable. Definitely time for a coffee."

The three of them sat on beanbags, conserving energy. Cameron had been working for almost twenty-four hours and was coming up to the wall of endurance. Sandeep and Joel were barely less tired, having snatched only a couple of hours' rest during the night.

"Let's leave the second subroutine for Ross," suggested

Joel. "As far as I can see, it's not doing any damage at the moment, and I'm knackered."

"Fair enough," replied Cameron. "I'll go and debrief Bill. The whole lot should be back up and running tomorrow. Do you guys want to do another sweep for breaches? Just make sure nothing's happened while we've been down here?"

Sandeep and Joel brightened.

"That's always fun to do," said Joel. "Okay, we'll get started."

•

Chief executive Sir Simon Winchester joined Cameron and Bill in the small meeting room that Cameron had first entered a full day earlier.

"I understand from Bill here that the worst is over."

"Yes, Sir Simon," replied Cameron. "As you already know, we managed to deliver the first global decryption for the visible ransomware overnight. This morning we assisted a team overseas to develop an antidote to the spread of the virus, effectively stopping it from downloading to new host computers. However, we have reason to believe the attack was tailing off already.

"Since then, we've isolated the first of two subroutines that were hidden behind the ransomware shell and which directly attacked the older operating systems in your bank."

Sir Simon looked from Cameron to Bill. "That all

sounds good, although most of it is beyond me. How long until we're up and running again?"

Cameron glanced at Bill and ploughed on. "Ross and the rest of the team will be back in shortly to work on isolating the second subroutine, tidy up the system, and compare the corrupted databases with the most recent clean backups. We'll then look to restore data to the most current version available. You should be good to boot up the whole network again early tomorrow morning, and we anticipate minimal loss of data overall."

Bill grinned, relieved, and Sir Simon nodded approvingly.

Cameron continued. "After that point, we can apply patches to the live system to protect against any recurrence of this specific threat and potentially stop similar routines in their tracks. We also need to identify the route of the original penetration and work with Bill to minimise future threats from the same source."

Cameron strongly suspected that the breach was due to human error, which meant there would be some retraining to be carried out for the staff: time to remind them of the implications of getting lax with emails. Bill caught Cameron's eye. He was obviously of the same opinion.

"We're indebted to you, Silvera," said Sir Simon. "Good job. Keep me in the loop on the reboot, Bill." He walked out of the meeting room and closed the door.

Cameron sighed. "I'll hand over to Ross at eight o'clock and go get some R&R. I need to be on my game for those patches, make sure we close up nice and tight." Pushing the heavy chair back on the carpet, Cameron stood up wearily.

Bill opened the door and the two of them strolled down the stairs.

As soon as they arrived in the operations room, there was a commotion. Sandeep called Cameron over to his monitor. "Good thinking running a new security scan. What prompted that, boss?"

Cameron blinked, and Bill looked puzzled. "Why, what have you found?"

Joel stepped forward, a bright white grin flashing across his dark features. "We picked up a new breach. It was very straightforward but occurred well after the attack started, around 10am today, and wasn't targeted at the background operating systems. We only caught it by chance. External login to the bank network, looks like an unsecured connection, and a sneaky little trojan slipped through. It's been broadcasting images from your CCTV, Bill. We closed it down straight away. We know whose account was compromised – a bit of security retraining needed there – but we haven't identified where those images have been sent. Not sure we ever will. Probably a little autocar around the corner that no one would notice. Now that the connection is down, they'll be long gone."

"I'll check the CCTV… Oh." Bill paused.

Sandeep finished his sentence for him. "If they could see your CCTV feeds, they'd make sure they couldn't be seen by the cameras."

Bill nodded, resigned. "We could approach other

networks locally but it's a busy district, and whoever they are they won't be obvious. Might even be in one of the adjoining buildings, out of sight. I wonder what they were after?"

•

Andy swore loudly as the CCTV feeds went blank. "Dammit. No more sightings. Have we got enough to go on?"

"Possibly." Andy looked up, hopeful. "We've sifted through the forum posts. Had to go back a lot longer than three months. This guy's careful. The business IP addresses match with the physical locations of known victims of cyber attacks over time; he hasn't tried to hide those. Interesting to see the range of places he's been working, though. Really high-profile stuff. Banks, data centres, power installations, all sorts."

Andy nodded. "This guy is the dog's. Top bloke. What about residential?"

"Nothing. The rest of the IP addresses are all over the place. Looks like he's simply been gaming them in the last year or so, changing to all sorts of mad locations from Patagonia to Iceland. Prior to that he was using one of the last VPNs to cloak his address, but the encryption on those is next to useless now. I guess he had to find a new way of hiding his whereabouts when going online."

"That makes sense. He goes out of his way to stay hidden, huh."

"Yes, Andy. It's almost as if he doesn't want you to find him." The surveillance guy sighed. He had his own opinions of the ethics of this investigation, but business was business.

"Okay, during the changeover from the VPN, we've picked up three posts, over a year ago, from a location just the other side of the river, near Borough tube station. That'll be your starting point."

Andy sat back, satisfied. "Okay, it's starting to come together. We think we know where this SimCavalier lives, or lived. We think we know what he looks like. Let's see if the pieces join up. Get Giles to stake him out."

•

Friday morning dawned, cool and clear. At the bank, Ross was ready to drop. Normally fit and on his game, the combination of long hours and the intense concentration needed to clean the databases had taken its toll. The strange anomaly in this worm worried him, too. There was something odd about the second subroutine, and try as he might he'd failed to crack it. He was looking forward to handing the reins back to the boss and getting some more sleep; maybe he'd be ready for a run later.

Ross admired his boss's talent, but resented playing second fiddle while his own career went nowhere. Cameron's flashes of insight and intuitive strategy were extraordinary, but there was a lot of hard graft from the whole team underneath. Ross believed he didn't always get the credit he deserved. Cameron's insistence on complete anonymity riled him. They were saving the world, weren't they? Surely he deserved a pat on the back, just occasionally? Some public recognition for a job well done?

"Another cuppa, Ross?" asked Susie, the new girl on the team.

Ross rubbed his face and ran a hand through his ginger hair. His grey eyes were bloodshot, his naturally pale skin looking wan in the artificial light. No more coffee. There was a limit to how much caffeine his system could take, especially with another race just two weeks away: the sensor on his wrist showed he was close to the maximum. Too much disruption too close to the start line, he reflected. Back in the day, cyber threats at this scale had appeared very rarely; the business generally ticked over doing steady nine to five digital training contracts, consultancy, and innocent security work to futureproof clients. That was perfect to keep his triathlon preparation steady. The last couple of years had been busier, and interruptions to his routine were increasingly unwelcome. With Cameron insisting on absolute discretion from the team, he had trouble concocting reasonable excuses time after time for his training partners.

"No," he replied curtly, feeling irritated and taking it out on the nearest person. He sighed. "Sorry Susie, tired out. Cameron and the other guys are on the way. They're bringing breakfast. Almost time for a kip. How's it going?"

"Baptism of fire, Ross," grinned Susie. "It's been a

challenge but I love it. Really tired though. Can't think straight any longer."

The door opened. Ross looked up as Cameron strolled in, looking refreshed and carrying an inviting, greasy paper bag, the smell of warm croissants drifting across the desk. "Breakfast as ordered, folks. Stand down, you've done a great job."

There was a scattered round of applause and a rustling of paper as five hungry pairs of hands made a grab for the pastries. Cameron let Ross enjoy the croissant, knowing it was one of his guilty pleasures in an otherwise strict regime. Once he'd reduced it to scant crumbs, the two of them slid out to talk in private in a meeting room on the other side of the hall.

"What's the anomaly you picked up in this code, then? There's not much you haven't seen before, Ross. What's got you so rattled?"

Ross slumped in his chair. "I'm not sure. It's what we thought was a second subroutine set to attack the systems. It doesn't appear to be executable – or rather, there is a piece of executable code in there, but it's completely unrelated to the original virus and is not triggered by any of the existing routines. It's code within code. It's almost as if the developer has annotated the virus code and then bundled it up in some obscure encryption to conceal the annotation. I can't get into it at all."

"Wow. That's pretty deep. You're absolutely sure it's not a secondary subroutine waiting to be triggered? Or something that's been released half-built?"

"Doesn't feel like it. It looks like a complete unit, no loose ends. There isn't anything I can find in the original code which would set it off. It categorically would not launch on its own as part of this attack." He paused, reflecting. "I think it needs human intervention. We don't have the key; somehow we need to get through the encryption. Run a quantum decryption, maybe?"

"Hmmm." Cameron thought for a moment. "If it's not part of this virus, what's its purpose? The Speakeasy creators would want the code to be as light as possible to avoid detection as it spread. There should be nothing in there that isn't functional. Most users won't pick up on this subroutine at all. The only people who'd ever see it would be teams like ours. No one else would be digging this deep into the virus. It's odd."

"I have a bad feeling about this." Ross stood up and stretched his back. "I'm going home to sleep on it. We're done. Susie's found the most likely penetration source and she can hand over to Sandeep. The database is clean and ready to restore. Good luck securing these godawful old systems. Over to you, boss."

Cameron smiled lopsidedly. "Sleep well. Back here for four to wrap up with the client. We should get our weekend after all."

•

Giles marched into the crowded office and headed for his desk. He plugged in his camera and set the images to upload, then walked across to the kitchen alcove where the coffee machine stood. A steaming cup of Americano was waiting for him. Technology was wonderful sometimes. He turned to see Andy approaching, and heard the machine behind him whirr into life again.

"How did you get on?"

"Some decent pics, I think," replied Giles. "Nice place he lives in. Must be doing okay for himself."

Andy laughed. "I think our 'SimCavalier' is hot property right now. Could probably afford to live at the Ritz judging by the volume of transactions going to that crypto wallet. Threat intelligence is big business."

The coffee machine sputtered as it dispensed a shot of espresso and diluted it with boiling water. Andy picked up his cup and the two men wandered over to Giles' desk. The monitor showed the first of the morning's images: a group of young professionals emerging from a building, smiling and talking. Slightly blurred to begin with, the focus sharpened as more images loaded.

Andy tapped the screen, indicating the young man in the grey hoodie. "Nice job, Giles." They scrolled through the series of images of the man, showing him walking to the main road, entering a shop, emerging with a bag in his hand.

"That's the lot. We got caught in the one-way system. Couldn't stop again. I think we have enough."

Andy flicked through the images again, zooming in

on the target. He frowned. "Let's compare these with the CCTV from the bank. Something doesn't look quite right." He shook his head. "No. It's got to be him. The IP trace for @SimCavalier definitely leads to that apartment block. Too much of a coincidence to get the same guy in two places."

"Want me to dig around the other occupants?" Andy shook his head.

"No, that's too random. We need to find out who his friends are. We can't risk frightening him off. He's been tough to pin down; thank goodness for that tipoff about the latest job. I don't understand why he doesn't come right out and take the credit. Me, I'd be shouting from the rooftops if I saved the world."

•

Deep in the bank, while Ross and his team were all home in bed, Cameron, Joel and Sandeep were ready to roll on the final phase. It was time to restore and secure the legacy systems.

Bill had joined them, keen to get the network back to life. He held his breath as the restored data flowed into the system, lines of records scrolling up the monitors faster than eye could follow.

"That's a beautiful sight," he sighed. "Ready to boot?"

"Yes. Go for it." Bill's own staff stepped in to bring the network back online, as Cameron turned to the team.

"Right, let's have a look at the source of infection, then

we can close up. What are the likely routes? What have we got so far? Sandeep?"

"Okay, Cameron, Susie pieced together most of this, and I've followed it up. She's done a good job. We've traced a file that came in on an email around six weeks ago. Bill and I have spoken to the guy who received it, first thing this morning. He can't really remember, but thinks he opened an attached document and found there was no content. Just assumed there was an error with the mail system. He expected the sender to fire it over again but never received anything and forgot all about it."

Bill continued. "We've had a look back through his mailbox. It was an executable file alright, and the sender wasn't who he thought it was. Phishing mail masquerading as a known contact from his address book. He's been with the bank for decades, and his HR record shows he's done the security training, but he simply didn't act on it. There's likely to be a disciplinary. He's been slack before. One of the old guard who doesn't always see the point of thinking before they click."

Cameron shrugged. "Human error. Always. Whether it's the individual, or the management not picking it up. So that was our virus? Are we sure?"

Sandeep nodded, confidently. "Yes, we've been over the rest of it with a fine-toothed comb. Apart from that odd little trojan yesterday morning, nothing else." He turned to Bill. "Really impressed. Great security. Pure bad luck on this one, I think."

Relieved, Bill stood up. "I'll go and let the Board know

that we're back up and running, and leave you to patch the rest."

It was done. Cameron sat in the silent room, satisfied. The archaic operating system was once more as tight as a drum. Out in the real world, people were charging wallets and drawing money as normal, the attack already forgotten as the weekend approached. Joel and Sandeep had already left; there was talk of a team night out to celebrate a job well done.

Cameron heard a knock at the door, and looked up as Ross walked in to the room. He seemed refreshed and much less pale, cheeks flushed from exercise, hair damp, casual in tracksuit and trainers.

"Good sleep? Good run?" asked Cameron.

Ross grinned. "Much better, thanks. Did the towpaths up to the Olympic Park, down the Lea and then round to Limehouse. I jumped on the train there, and took advantage of the showers here in the bank. Blew the cobwebs away nicely. How's it going?"

"Pretty much sorted. Back end secure and we know how it got in. Some training to do over the next few weeks. I haven't touched that hidden code, just surgically removed it. Let's go and wrap up with the Board. It's payday."

•

Cameron and Ross once again shook hands with Sir Simon Winchester, handed back their security passes, and walked out of the building.

"Another one bites the dust," said Ross with satisfaction.

Cameron nodded. "Could have been whole lot worse. It was a pretty straightforward takedown once we cracked the routine."

"Once you cracked it," corrected Ross.

Cameron looked wryly at him. "Team effort, man. Couldn't do it without you."

They were silent for a moment. It had been an odd job. The malicious code had been unusually simple to disable, in the end. The hidden routine was still a mystery, despite cleaning up the rest of the virus. Cameron had isolated the odd code and planned to work on it in quarantine. First, however, there were more important things to deal with. Time to get back into normal life.

"What've you got planned for the weekend, then? Racing?"

Ross shook his head. "Next big one is two weeks away. I need to get back on track with my training. This job came along at the wrong time. Can't be helped. You?"

"Family calls. Big brother throwing a knees-up. It's Sameena's fortieth and everyone is descending on the village. It'll be good to take a break."

Ross laughed. "That'll be a first. You never switch off. Taking the new fella along?"

Cameron reddened. "Nope. I think it would be too much of a shock to the system. And anyway, he's strictly recreational right now. I don't want Charlie to think I'm settling down."

Ross dragged his grey hoodie over his head as the

afternoon air cooled. The two of them strolled towards the station. From the shadows, a figure watched them until they turned out of sight.

•

Cameron opened the apartment door and the cat miaowed an ecstatic greeting. Otherwise, all was silent.

"Lights." The glow illuminated a tidy kitchen/diner, washing up done and put away, and a note on the table next to a bowl of fresh apples. "Cam, hope the training went well, enjoy your weekend – Ben. PS. I fed the cat."

Cameron sighed, and glared at the cat which was protesting starvation. It would have been good to have Ben along this weekend, but letting the whole tribe loose on him at once would be unfair. The kids were curious enough but Aunt Vicky was another matter. Mandisa would be sorry not to meet him, though. She was dying for news of her best friend's latest conquest and had been badgering Cameron for the last two weeks for an introduction. It would have to wait.

Too tired to meet up with the rest of the team, but not in the mood to travel this evening, Cameron threw country clothes and smarts into a bag and set an early alarm. Lying on the bed in the dark, the cat purring, that hidden code continued to niggle.

It was no use. The mystery had to be solved.

The cyber communities were abuzz with speculation. Cameron set the apartment's IP address mask to a random point on the globe, and logged in to join the chatter. As much as their work was serious, these professionals scattered across the world were all friends, and they provided each other with a lot of light relief through snide observations and clever in-jokes. Today's posts ranged from the serious work of sorting the Speakeasy attack, through a long discussion of the sleeping habits of cats, to the mystery of the second subroutine.

Cameron skimmed the thread about cats, laughed out loud at couple of posts, uploaded a picture of the little black and white cat curled up in an impossibly tortuous position with a toy mouse clutched between its paws, and then turned to the hidden code discussion.

"Hey guys, what've we got so far?"

There was a chorus of welcome.

"SimCavalier, you back! How you doing?"

"Where've you been hiding?"

"You cracked it already?"

"Been busy, guys. Thought you'd have broken it by now. You been asleep? Spend all your time taking pictures of cats? I leave you alone for a few hours and look what happens."

A gale of laughter was accompanied by posted snippets of film, old gifs that still made users laugh. "We've been waiting for you to ride in and fix it, SimCavalier. We brought popcorn."

Cameron grinned broadly. "Seriously guys, where are we? I promise not to take all the credit."

There was a ripple of amusement. "Yeah, you're not

RunningManTech. You play fair. Where's he got to, anyway? Haven't seen him on here for days. He's not answering threads."

"RunningManTech is running, what did you think he'd be doing? He's got a race coming up. Training before pleasure. C'mon, let's have a look at this. I'm tired."

Cameron pushed the code dump up to the forum. "Say what you see. Looks pretty straightforward from here, you useless lot. Line 24 refers back to a web address, liberatorseven.com, anything there?"

"Yeah, it exists, but it's parked. The ICANN listing's pretty funny."

Cameron brought the details of the rogue domain up on the screen, and laughed.

"It's a homage to old-school sci-fi. Well, I thought they had a sense of humour when I saw the Speakeasy gif. Look at this… 'Registrant J-L Picard, 1701 Tribble Street, Enterprise Town, Nevada… Phone 702-474-571'. That's classic."

"Keep reading," came a post. "It gets better."

Cameron scanned further down the listing.

"Whaaa…? 'Tech contact Z Beeblebrox' – seriously? This got through ICANN? – '42 Magratheasgata, Trondheim… Phone 72-26-7709'. Love it."

Cameron paused. "This is all a lot of fun, but why? Why go to all this trouble? Let's have a look at the source code again."

The chatter died down as the forum members pored over the lines of code. Cameron was thinking hard: it made no sense. The little programme did not appear to hide anything, and had not run in the attack.

It hadn't run.

What would happen if it ran?

"Has anyone tried running this routine?"

"Yeah, of course, it's a dead end. Check it out." Cameron turned to the quarantine computer, a stripped-back operating system linked to nothing at all. The code was already loaded there for examination.

'Run.'

On screen, a single box appeared. 'Password?' it said.

Cameron snapped an image of the monitor with the smartscreen camera, and uploaded it to the forum.

"This what you all got?"

"Yeah. Pretty odd stuff for a bundle of malicious code."

"Is that what it is? It didn't attack anything. Sure, it was delivered as part of an attack, but it stayed dormant. We are the only people who have seen it. Maybe we are the people who were meant to run it."

"So what's the password, genius?"

"That's the big question, isn't it, guys," replied Cameron. "Okay. I'm sure this routine has been written for us to find. The only people who'd see it and get this far are nerds like us. Look at all the references. The password has to be something that links us all. Chuck me some ideas."

"More sci-fi references? Spaceships?"

"TARDIS, Rocinante, Heart of Gold, Sleeper Service…"

"Millennium Falcon," came another post.

"Red Dwarf. Serenity..."

"Nope, nothing yet. Give me a second, just pulling a routine together to test all possibilities in that genre. What other terms would all of us know? It can't be too random, it's relying on shared context in the threat intelligence field."

"Cyberattacks, viruses, worms? Speakeasy. WannaCry. ILoveYou. Chairmaker. EternalPetya. Mirai. Morris..."

"Running those now... No, nothing."

"How about us?"

"What do you mean?"

"Our handles. Feed all our handles in and see what you get." There was a wave of chatter, and then silence, a virtual in-drawing of breath.

Cameron ran the routine, testing the names of all the forum members faster than human eye could follow.

Nothing.

No, wait. One name would not be on the list. The user who generated it.

Barely breathing, Cameron typed slowly into the box on the screen: 'SimCavalier'.

The box flashed green and disappeared. The screen went dark. Plain white text appeared.

'Batten down the hatches for hurricane season.'

4: HOMECOMING

Another early morning, but this time Cameron felt relaxed, if not particularly well rested. After the revelations of the hidden subroutine, the release of sleep had been slow to come, with disturbing dreams of giant worms and server stacks, swirling storms, and the shining sword of a cavalier.

Rain had fallen overnight, and the air was damp and cool. Leaving the cat with enough food to feed a feline army, Cameron grabbed the overnight bag and walked steadily down the deserted staircase to the quiet, pre-dawn dark of the street, heading straight to the underground station. The Northern Line shuttle to Euston was just pulling in to the platform. Fifteen minutes later, Cameron emerged onto the station concourse and scanned the departure listings. The next train out towards Milton Keynes and Birmingham was leaving in a quarter of an hour; plenty of time to buy a coffee before heading down the ramp to board.

The train emerged into the early morning daylight, slowly winding through North London towards Watford and beyond, passing Wembley Stadium, its famous arch dominating the skyline, white metal shining against the rich, dark colours of the dawn sky. As buildings gave way to trees and fields, the carriage picked up speed, a short crescendo in the steady electric hum. Cameron leant against the window, hypnotised by the familiar rhythm of the wheels on the tracks. The sun was rising; it cast a pale, yellow light over the countryside. Small towns and farms, fields and villages, flew by, a patchwork of countryside that Cameron knew by heart. The train crossed a bridge over the Grand Union Canal; there was little pleasure boat traffic at this time of day, but plenty of freight barges were already on the move, shipping goods slowly up the country on the ancient network of waterways.

Purring to a stop, the train disgorged a handful of passengers. Cameron strolled through the small station and out of the main doors, where a fleet of autocars waited patiently at charging points. The For Hire sign on a small autocar lit up as it sensed passing trade. Cameron climbed in, stowed the bag, told the taxi the address, and thumbed its payment button. The little cab waited until the seatbelt locked, then pulled out towards the road.

Cameron relaxed, enjoying the ride. They crossed the river and left the town behind, skirting the hill where Iron Age man once built his fort, and Twentieth Century man built dormitory suburbs. The empty dual carriageway crossed a silent motorway, and for a while followed the line of a branch of the canal, white-painted locks in motion as deliveries arrived at local depots. A few kilometres further on, the cab turned off the main road and drove steadily down a leafy village lane to the house Cameron had grown up in, which was now home to Charlie and his lively family.

Cameron climbed out of the vehicle, retrieved her bag, and sent the little autocar back to its lair. Straightening up, she braced herself as a whirlwind of children and an excitable dog arrived at speed.

"Aunty Cam! Aunty Cam! Daddy, Daddy, Aunty Cam's here!"

Charlie ambled up and extricated Cameron from the sea of hugs. "Hi little sis, good trip?" He kissed her warmly on the cheek, took her bag and they walked together towards the house. "Sorry you couldn't get here last night – busy time at work, I guess." Cameron nodded, and Charlie grimaced. "We got a hit from the same virus. No – don't worry," he continued hurriedly, as she looked concerned, "our own systems weren't compromised; you've done a great job there. Lost our printers for almost a day thanks to a breach at the main data centre, took a while for them to be sure they could restore backups safely. Luckily, we're covered for cyber attack interruption. No problem with the insurers, especially as the in-house systems are so tight."

Cameron smiled. "Good to hear our defences are holding. Nasty little virus, did a fair bit of short-term damage, but we caught it at our end and it looks like the fix we developed neutralised the threat globally. Great work from Ross and the team."

"How's Ross doing?" asked Charlie. "And why would Mandisa be asking me if you're bringing someone to the party? New boyfriend?"

"Ross is fine, his usual grumpy self, does a good job, but only happy when he's running, swimming, biking or all three. Any rumours of a new boyfriend are strictly unconfirmed and not to reach Aunt Vicky under any circumstances, okay?"

Charlie laughed. Aunt Vicky was their mother's only sister. In her seventies now, she still lived in the village, and had kept a close eye on her niece and nephew since their parents' untimely passing. Cameron was hoping to keep Ben off her radar for now.

Entering the old farmhouse kitchen, the tail end of breakfast was evident. Plates, spoons, jars of jam, cartons of milk, and empty cups were scattered on the wooden table in the centre of the kitchen. The children had scampered off as soon as there was a hint of a chore to be done, and Sameena was alone, stacking the dishwasher and gradually clearing the table.

Cameron walked over to her sister-in-law and gave her a hug. "Happy Birthday, Sameena. Are you all set for the party?"

Sameena put down a jam-covered plate and laughed. "Nowhere near ready, Cam, neither for the party nor for being forty. I just want to pretend I am thirty again. Is that allowed?" She shook her head ruefully for a moment, then smiled broadly. "You are in your usual room, we haven't kicked you out yet. Waiting for you to settle down first. Nina is after that attic, mind. She is growing up far too fast. Secondary school next year – can you believe it?"

Cameron could. Nina had shot up over the past couple

of years, obviously bestowed with the long legs and slim build of the Silvera women. Bright and academic, she had Charlie and Cameron's dark hair, and her mother's coffee-coloured skin and brown eyes. Her precocious intelligence was being matched by emerging beauty.

"There may be trouble ahead," sang Cameron under her breath.

Dilan and Tara marched into the kitchen, squabbling over a toy. "Mum, it's my turn. Tara grabbed it off me!"

Sameena sighed and turned to deal with the fight.

Cameron took her chance to grab a slice of toast from the table, and spread it with jam, suddenly hungry after the last few days of disrupted routine.

Charlie laughed as he came into the room. "You have jam all over your face, Cam. Nothing changes. Want a coffee?"

Cameron shook her head. "Toast will do, thanks. What's the plan for today? Can I do anything?"

"I think we're organised, love. Caterers will be here by noon, they'll do all the heavy lifting. You relax. You've had a hard week. I've put your bag upstairs."

"Thanks, Charlie. I said I'd meet Mandisa for a drink before lunch. I'll take Roxy out for a walk, keep her out from under everyone's feet. Is that okay?"

Charlie smiled gratefully. "Good plan. Say hi to Mandisa. She's coming this afternoon, isn't she?"

"Oh yes," replied Cameron, nodding, "but we need a good gossip without Aunt Vicky listening in." She winked at Charlie, who laughed knowingly.

Cameron finished her toast, and headed upstairs to unpack her bag. Climbing a hidden staircase to the top floor, she emerged into her attic domain, which extended almost the full length of the house. Walls angled inwards with the steep pitch of the roof, low to the floor at the skirting boards. Three bright dormer windows faced south. The view over the green fields was as breath-taking as ever; a line of dark trees and hedges showed where the brook babbled between fields, and in the distance sheep were grazing. Cameron's bedroom was partitioned off at one end. Faded, once brightly patterned, wallpaper still decorated the attic. Real paper books were ranged on low shelves under the sloping eaves. A threadbare teddy sat by the bed, framed, printed photographs and a scrap metal salamander hung on the wall. A PC sat on an old desk, with twin monitors mounted on brackets. A router stood on a small cabinet next to the desk, dormant, no lights flashing. In the corner, a pile of older hardware and jumbled wires was gathering dust. On a shelf, in pride of place, lay her mother's old ZX81, the family's first home computer, useless without its monitor and cassette player. Those were lurking in a cupboard, and hadn't seen the light of day for over a decade.

Cameron unpacked her bag, hanging her dress in the small wardrobe ready for the afternoon's celebrations. She unearthed a treat for the kids, and the gift she'd bought for Sameena weeks ago; she was so glad she hadn't left shopping until the last minute.

Next, she plugged in the PC and router, changing the

admin passwords as a matter of course, using a new combination from the generator on her smartscreen. Checking her mailbox, there were no urgent messages to deal with.

The forums were filled with speculation on the strange result of cracking the hidden code, but Cameron chose not to log on just now. That could wait. The best brains in the world were puzzling over its significance. For Cameron, a greater challenge awaited. It was time to face the children. She took a deep breath and headed downstairs into the fray.

Sameena looked relieved when Cameron allowed the kids to bear her off to the family room. Dilan and Tara headed straight for the computer. The monitor hung on the wall, facing the room. Anything they did, every site they accessed, could be seen by passing adults. There was little temptation to disappear down online rabbit holes, and plenty of scope to show off.

"Cameron, look what I did." Tara tapped on a file and the screen was suddenly full of tumbling unicorns, turning cartwheels across the pink background as stars and sparkles flew. "I made it all by myself."

Dilan snorted with derision. At eight, the simple programming his little sister loved was beneath him, although Cameron clearly remembered his own similar early attempts, featuring dancing dinosaurs and exploding meteors.

Nina had followed them in, but was sitting apart,

sulking, a smartscreen dangling in her hand. "Mum won't let me have today's wifi password."

"Come and sit with us," offered Cameron. "I've got a challenge for you. And anyway, it's the party this afternoon, your mum doesn't want you creeping off to a corner with that screen and ignoring everyone." Nina grumbled, but put down the screen and joined her aunt and siblings at the computer.

Cameron dropped a pre-prepared file from her smartscreen over to the PC. "Right kids, code cracking time. There's a hidden message in this graph – what treat have I brought for you? There's also a key to what each of the points in the graph could mean. Trouble is, there are 256 possibilities for each one. Do you think you can crack the message before lunch?"

Tara looked worried, but Nina rolled her eyes. "Aunty Cam, that's way too easy. Just need to process all the possibilities and watch the spikes."

Cameron laughed. "It's one thing to know the theory, another to run it. Get going. Get the answer, and you'll get the treat. And it has to be all three of you working as a team."

She sat back, smiling, as her nieces and nephew fought for position in front of the monitor. Gradually they settled to work together, Nina explaining the process to Dilan, and Tara watching the patterns. That'll keep them out of Sameena's hair for an hour or so, she thought.

Relaxing on the familiar old sofa, Cameron gazed

around the walls at family photos, printed and framed treasures as well as scrolling digital displays. High up, away from direct sunlight, were the black and white portraits of her own grandparents and great-grandparents, stiff and formal, holding still for the photographer to avoid blurring the precious negative. The pictures of her parents were more relaxed, smiling on holiday, smart at a wedding, and laughing in a family portrait with Cameron as a toddler and Charlie aged about ten.

Lower down were informal images of Cameron and Charlie, and of Sameena with her brothers and sisters, every moment of their childhoods captured in digital colour. Digital screens scrolled pictures from the last decade of the three dark-haired youngsters now huddled around the monitor. So many changes in the past century, reflected Cameron. Even her own grandmother had barely scratched the surface of the burgeoning digital world. Now, the world was almost entirely digital, just fifty years after the World Wide Web came into existence.

She dozed in her warm nest on the old sofa, relaxing properly for the first time in days.

A cheer went up from the children. Cameron started awake and checked her watch. "Seventy-three minutes. Not bad at all. What's the answer?"

"Chocolate," squealed Tara.

Cameron grinned, and produced a small parcel.

"Off you go. Enjoy." She yawned and stretched, clambered off the sofa, and closed down the screen as the kids ran outside. Time to go and meet Mandisa. It would be good to see her friend again.

•

Cameron escaped out of the back door and walked around the side of the house, feeling the crunch of familiar gravel beneath her feet. Roxy the Labradoodle bounced around her madly, wagging her blonde tail so hard that her hindquarters danced, anticipating a proper walk. The early spring snowdrops and crocuses in the lawn were over, a few sad green spikes all that remained of the colourful display. A host of bright yellow daffodils nestled under the hedge and surrounded the base of the lilac trees. No blossom yet; spring was further ahead in the city. The bleat of lambs carried on a light breeze from the fields opposite the house. Cameron clipped Roxy's leash to her collar and set off out of the gate.

The village had hardly changed since her childhood, and probably very little since her mother's childhood, either. There had been a village here for a millennium. In 1068, the Domesday Book recorded two households, five ploughlands and seven acres of woodland, farmed by Saxon lords under the tenancy of Count Robert of Mortain. It had grown since those times, but remained small.

Rounding the corner, Cameron skirted a limestone wall and passed the neat gardens of a row of cottages, once home to the workers at a nearby farm. The street opened up onto the village green, bordered on the far side by the same small brook, and deserted but for another distant dog walker. Cameron smiled as she remembered the hot summers of her childhood. She and her friends spent days dressed in swimming costumes and sandals, playing in the clear shallow water, trying to catch young sticklebacks which slipped through their fingers and away downstream. The green still hosted sports day for the tiny village school that stood opposite, where Charlie, then Cameron, and now the three children, had first studied their reading, writing, 'rithmetic, and Ruby. Eight years older than his sister, Charlie had spent those summers acting cool rather than staying cool, hanging out with his older friends well away from the embarrassing little kids.

The road meandered up a small rise, topped by the ancient square tower of a pretty limestone church. Cameron gave a passing nod to the place; her parents and grandparents had been laid to rest in that churchyard, and she would pay her respects later. Behind the church she could see workers in the vineyard checking the buds for emerging flower clusters. A small private vineyard had once thrived there, but as the world warmed, vines became big business, changing the focus of centuries of local agriculture. Now the fields were all planted in thin, dark rows, providing Chardonnay and Pinot Gris to the great champagne houses whose traditional lands were increasingly barren.

The road narrowed, and Cameron shivered slightly in the shadow of a row of great horse-chestnut trees. Up ahead she could see the welcoming sign of the village pub, the social hub for everything from Friday nights to funerals. Cameron reached the old white building, opened the gate, and crossed the small beer garden, exchanging greetings in passing with a couple of pre-lunch drinkers. She tied Roxy up to an empty wooden picnic table and entered the porch of the pub, stepping down, blinking, into a small wooden-beamed bar. Sitting on a stool, gossiping with the landlord, was Mandisa.

"Caaaaaameron," she squealed. "Where's the new boyfriend then?" Mandisa hopped off the stool and gave her friend a hug, peering behind her at the door, hoping to see another figure entering.

Cameron laughed ruefully. "I'm sorry. I didn't think he was ready for the Spanish Inquisition. We'll have to get together in London instead. I'm less busy now, thank goodness. All quiet on the Western Front." She tapped her nose conspiratorially. After ten years in the business, she still managed to keep her front-line role a secret from all but her closest friends and family. Even Ben, bless him, thought she simply delivered training and advice on cyber security. She wondered what he'd made of the last few days, and their broken dates, early mornings, and late nights.

"I'll have a half, please, and a bowl of water for the dog." Cameron sighed. "Total chaos at home. Last minute organisation and caterers everywhere. Madness. It's great to get out for an hour; I used the dog as an excuse."

Mandisa laughed. "I bet the kids aren't helping at all."

"Well, they think they are. Nina's not so bad, she has her head screwed on and she's growing up fast, but Dilan and Tara are driving Sameena mad. I've done my morning shift as the good aunt and this is my statutory break. At least I'll have you as reinforcements this afternoon."

Nodding to the landlord, Cameron and Mandisa took their drinks out to the beer garden, Cameron ducking as she stepped through the door. "Number of times I've banged my head coming up that step…" she grumbled.

"Your fault for growing so tall," chided Mandisa. "I told you to stop when we were eleven. Is the weather good up there? Can you reach the high shelf for me?"

Cameron good-naturedly flicked a drop of beer at her friend. "Not fair. Not my fault. Short arse."

The dog walker from the green had made it all the way up the village. Off her leash, Roxy's tail wagged like a demented metronome, spying a friend. The two dogs snuffled at each other and splashed as they drank their water. Cameron and Mandisa said hello to the new arrival; not someone they knew, an incomer to the village, but apparently long enough established for the dogs to be acquainted.

"You're Charlie's sister, aren't you? Down from London for the party, eh?"

Cameron nodded.

"Andrew. Andrew Taylor. I live up the hill. Nice to meet you. Shame you're not here more often. I commute up, it's just as easy as trying to cross London."

"Ah, too quiet here. Much more fun in the capital

for now, Andrew. So, you know Charlie, then? Are you coming along this afternoon?"

"Call me Andy. I think the whole village is invited." He looked enquiringly at Mandisa. "Sorry, you are…?"

"Old schoolfriend. I only live the other side of the town. Mandisa Menzi. I'll be there too." She extended her hand.

Andy shook Mandisa's hand, and looked curiously at Cameron. "I'm sure we've met before, somewhere."

Cameron shrugged. "I don't think so, Andy."

Andy frowned, something niggling at the back of his mind. "Must be the family resemblance. Young Nina is the double of you, Cameron."

Cameron smiled. "Yes, she's growing up fast." She finished her drink. "We'd better get going. I promised to wear this beastie out and she needs a good run on the field. Nice to meet you, Andy. See you this afternoon." Roxy trotted over obediently and Cameron re-attached her leash. Mandisa took the glasses back in to the bar, and they set off out of the garden again and turned to go further up the lane.

Andy watched them go, puzzled, then ducked into the pub.

•

The party was in full swing. Long tables laden with food lined a shady stone terrace in the angle of the house. Discreet caterers passed among the crowd on the terrace and lawn, replenishing glasses and collecting plates. Children ran around squealing, playing in the longer grass away from the adults. Nina had forgotten her grown-up pose and lack of smartscreen, and was joining in the fun with visiting cousins and local friends. Cameron and Mandisa exchanged gossip with villagers they had known from school days, gathering news of old friends who had moved away. A couple of Charlie and Sameena's university friends were gamely chatting up the two girls, amused that the little sister they remembered had grown into an elegant, self-confident woman.

Cameron glanced across the lawn and spotted her elderly aunt. She was holding forth with tales of bygone times and the latest village gossip, fuelled by local fizz, but Cameron could tell even from a distance that Aunt Vicky was not on her usual sparkling form. Excusing herself from the laughing group, Cameron caught her aunt at the groaning buffet table in search of more nibbles. "What's up, Aunt Vicky?"

"Oh Cameron, darling, it's the cat." She sounded upset. Cameron wondered what had happened to the evil fluffball this time. The old cat that Cameron grew up with had been a sleek, elegant, black tom with impeccable manners. You could leave a slice of ham on the table and the cat would not so much as sniff at it. There was an easy truce with all the neighbouring cats, and he spent sunny days outside on the porch making friends with every visitor and every passer-by.

That was years ago, and Bob the cat was long gone.

Aunt Vicky had subsequently acquired a long-haired ginger beast of dubious provenance by the name of Donald. Donald stalked the garden, dug up the seedlings in the vegetable patch, fought with Boris the tabby next door, and regularly got himself stuck up trees in pursuit of feathered prey, from where his loyal staff would rescue him.

"The poor baby is ill," (oh that's a shame, thought Cameron) "and when I contacted the vet, they said they could treat him, but it sounded like a pre-existing condition, and his pet insurance won't cover the costs. He may need an operation – it could be thousands. What am I going to do?"

Cameron could think of several answers to this question, none of which were particularly diplomatic or comforting. She discarded 'Good riddance' and 'Don't waste your money' for the kinder option.

"Poor Donald. He's had a wonderful pampered life. What is he, fourteen? That's well over seventy in cat years. I'm sure he'll be fine. You can't expect him to be on top form at that age – present company excepted, of course." Cameron had her fingers crossed behind her back. Had she managed to navigate the fine line?

Aunt Vicky snuffled sadly. "Yes dear, I suppose you're right. When I adopted him, he was in such a state I didn't expect him to last four years, let alone eight. Oh, the worry he's caused me."

"Come on, Aunt Vicky, chin up. This is Sameena's day. You can worry about Donald tomorrow. Have another glass of fizz. Can't believe the weather, can you? Lovely for the time of year."

Cameron steered her aunt to the nearest smiling caterer and picked up two glasses. She thought about providing some distraction from cat woes by dropping a hint about the new boyfriend, but before she could put her foot firmly in her mouth, she heard a voice behind her.

"Afternoon Vicky, how are you? Haven't seen your Donald over our fence recently. Boris thinks all his Christmases have come at once."

Aunt Vicky's face lit up. "Andy, how lovely to see you. Have you met my niece, Cameron? Cameron, this is my next-door neighbour. He works up in London too."

"I met your lovely niece this morning, Vicky, when I was out walking Jasper. Hello Cameron. We've definitely met before somewhere, just can't place it." He smiled broadly, but his eyes were narrowed and searching.

"Hello Andy," replied Cameron cautiously. "I'm still sure we haven't met. I didn't realise you were Aunt Vicky's new neighbour. When did you move in?"

"Arrived at the end of last year. Beautiful spot. Easy distance to the city. Of course, I can work here at home too, so convenient since they upgraded the village connections."

Aunt Vicky nodded enthusiastically. "Oh yes, it's lovely to have neighbours in the village during the day. In the old days, unless you worked on the farm, everyone commuted. The place was deserted. Much more fun now."

Andy was not to be deterred. "What is it you do down in London, Cameron?"

"Oh – I work in robotics – nothing exciting – training and so on. I have to be there in person, no chance of doing it from here. What about you?" Cameron smiled sociably, but something didn't feel right. There was nothing outwardly threatening about this unassuming man, but he was watching her a little too closely for a casual acquaintance. She glanced around for an escape, and saw Mandisa coming across the lawn towards her. As Andy opened his mouth to reply, Cameron hurriedly butted in.

"Sorry, Aunt Vicky, Andy, we have something to sort out for the birthday girl." She stepped forward to meet Mandisa, and they turned around to head for the house. Cameron could feel Andy's eyes boring into her back.

"He gives me the creeps," said Mandisa. "I don't know what it is, but I don't like him."

Cameron nodded. She trusted her sixth sense. It was what made her good at her job, after all. She needed to know more about this Andrew Taylor. Leaving Mandisa in the kitchen, she dashed up to the attic and fired a quick encrypted message to Ross. "Andrew Taylor, late forties, average everything, lives in my village, moved here last summer, works in London, cat Boris, dog Jasper, no family. Might be tough to track, common name, but any dirt?" If there was any basis to her gut instinct, Ross would find out.

Cameron slipped back downstairs clutching the gift

for Sameena, just as a splendid birthday cake was being positioned on a small table in the middle of the lawn. Staying well away from the mysterious Mr Taylor, she and Mandisa joined a cluster of friends and family to sing Happy Birthday. Glowing, Sameena cut into the cake, Charlie proposed a toast to his wife, glasses clinked, and the cake was whisked away for cutting. Mandisa disappeared into the kitchen again and acquired two slices, handing one to Cameron.

Cameron sighed. "Ah, a slice won't hurt. I feel like I've eaten enough for the whole weekend already this afternoon. After the last few days I need to get back to training."

Mandisa laughed. "No, girl, what you need is a holiday. You work too hard. What say we have a week away? Go and find some sunshine?"

Cameron brightened. "That's a nice idea. I have a bunch of training booked in, and there is a loose end to tidy from this latest job. If it's quiet after that then yes, take me away."

The cool spring evening was growing dark as the sun set behind the house. Guests were starting to take their leave, and the crowd thinned out as they left in twos and threes, most on foot, some by autocar back to other villages, the local town, and the station. The chattering voices of other children faded. Nina appeared, carrying a tired Tara, and followed by Dilan dragging a large stick.

Cameron took charge of them, gently persuading Dilan to give up his stick and leave it on the terrace for the night. She hustled the younger two to their bedrooms while Nina wandered off to join her parents for an hour or so, claiming the privilege of a later bedtime. Tara, resplendent in Tigger pyjamas and clutching a cuddly panda, snuggled up in her bed, asleep before her head hit the pillow. Dilan insisted he wasn't tired, resisting every effort to tuck him in, but when Cameron checked on him a few minutes later, he was out for the count.

•

Andrew Taylor frowned as he climbed the hill towards his house. Where had he seen that girl before? It wasn't simply the family resemblance to Charlie and Nina that had triggered this half-baked recollection. He had seen her recently, this week, in another context.

Boris the cat arrived at the door with him, yowling for food after a day protecting his territory, or sleeping in the warmest spot in the garden, more like. Inside, Jasper trotted up to greet him, tail wagging. Andy fed them both, distracted, puzzling over the mystery. He thought through his week. Had he seen her out in London? Had she been in the office? Sitting on the same train? No, he couldn't place her anywhere. Why was this niggling so much?

Frustrated, Andy switched on his computer and glanced at the job he'd been working on this morning. Two sets of photographs, one grainy and almost monochrome, one high resolution colour. Images of the same man, his quarry.

Andy scrolled through the CCTV images. He could see the man entering a lobby, walking to reception. In the next image, his back was to the camera, the hood of his sweatshirt hanging down, as he spoke to the receptionist. A later image picked up his features as he left the building: white, pale, short hair. Dark? Hard to tell.

Andy flicked to the other set of images. The same man walking away from the camera in the morning sunlight. Height, build, hoodie the same. Blond hair. Hmm. That could be a trick of the light. Scrolling back through the photos for a full-face image, Andy cursed at he realised the first three or four snaps of the man leaving the apartment were just out of focus. He really wasn't having any luck.

Suddenly, something caught his eye. He zoomed in to the group of young people leaving the apartment, his quarry's face blurred, but others clear.

Andy sat back, stunned. That was where he'd seen her before. Charlie's sister lived in the same apartment block as the man he was stalking. She had left home at the same time yesterday morning, and had been caught on camera by Andy's staff. Finally, he had a lead to the SimCavalier.

5: RUN AND HIDE

Cameron woke early again. The morning sun was streaming through the blinds that hung on the dormer window. She yawned and stretched, luxuriating in the pleasure of a rare morning where nothing needed to be done. The house was quiet, the children still asleep, exhausted after the fun of the party.

An old red dressing gown hung on a hook by the wardrobe. Cameron threw it on over her pyjamas and padded down the attic stairs, opening the door to the main landing quietly. The click of the latch alerted Roxy, and Cameron heard the dog's claws tapping on the old flagstones of the hallway below, as she too stretched and rose from sleep.

The kitchen was a mess. No one had bothered to tidy at the end of the night, although the debris of the afternoon's catering had been neatly removed. Cameron filled the kettle and clicked it on to boil. The switch was stiff with lack of use, the kettle tuned in to the activity and biorhythms and apps of the household.

She opened the fridge, and jumped as a disembodied voice addressed her. "Good morning. The milk is almost out of date. Shall I order some more? You have an offer to change brand, would you like to hear it?"

Cameron paused, then replied clearly, "Order four litres, same brand."

"Order placed," came the reply. "Delivery in eighteen minutes."

Cameron lifted out the old milk carton and sniffed at it anyway. Seems fine, she thought. The kettle boiled. Cameron threw a teabag into the large mug that Nina had printed for her when she was little, poured in the water, and let the bag stew for a few minutes while she absent-mindedly stacked plates and glasses by the dishwasher. Adding a splash of milk, Cameron returned the carton to the fridge, closing the door quickly to stop it talking.

She opened the back door to let Roxy run out in the garden. It was cloudy, and too cold to settle down outside, so Cameron wandered through to the family room and curled up on the sofa. A movement caught her eye at the window; the milk drone had arrived. She got up quickly and went to the front door to collect the cartons and put them away, hoping that Charlie and Sameena wouldn't be disturbed by the delivery drone's arrival.

It was peaceful in the sleeping house, and Cameron's mind wandered as she reflected on the events of the past week. The job at the bank had ultimately been simple, but the long hours had taken more out of her than she expected. The mystery of the message hidden in the subroutine of the Speakeasy virus added a layer of concern, a niggle at the back of her mind.

She would head back to London this afternoon, she

decided, and spend some time with Ben. He was a sweet guy, and funny, and great in bed: she liked him a lot. She would plan the next round of training with Bill at the bank, and organise her diary to get a girls' week away very soon with Mandisa. She would stop worrying about the mysterious Mr Taylor, and the meaning of the cryptic message. Life would settle into its normal routine, until the next time.

Fine intentions. But Cameron's competitive streak and love of a mystery would ultimately win. She needed to know what the message meant. She wanted to get there before everyone else. However hard she tried to relax, it would draw her back in the end.

She sighed. Today she would reserve for herself, her family, and her friends. Tomorrow was another matter.

The door opened, and Charlie wandered in. "You're up early. I heard the milk come. Another cuppa?"

Cameron smiled. "Go on, then." She handed Charlie her empty mug.

"News channel," muttered Charlie into thin air as he wandered back out towards the kitchen. A screen on the wall glowed, and the mellifluous tones of the hosts of the Sunday morning news and discussion programmes washed over Cameron as she sat, deep in thought. Snippets of news stories drifted in and out of her consciousness. "…last breeding pair of polar bears in the wild… earliest recorded full melt of Arctic floes…" "…thirty-eighth annual drone racing championship underway at Alexandra Palace…" "…sterling strengthens against the Bitcoin… cyber hero applauded following successful code cracking…"

Charlie reappeared with tea and toast. He put the tray down on the small table, straightened, and looked at screen, astonished. "Cameron – isn't that Ross?"

Cameron looked up, open-mouthed, as the newscaster continued.

"…foiled the so-called 'Speakeasy' cyberattack this week. These first pictures show the threat intelligence operative known only as the SimCavalier riding to the rescue when the virus struck on Wednesday. He has been hailed as a hero, and there are calls to recognise his contribution to maintaining the security of…"

"Pause," shouted Cameron. "Go back thirty seconds." She stared at the screen. The first grainy picture clearly showed Ross standing alone in the foyer of the bank.

Cameron laughed incredulously. "That's where we were this week. That's Ross, you're right, but they're talking about me." She was suddenly sober. "Charlie, this is really bad. No one has ever gotten close to identifying any of us. I've been doing this for almost ten years. And now, they've found the team – if not me – and they know my handle. What the hell is going on?"

"Cam, love, that's manageable. I know you want to stay anonymous, but if they haven't identified you then you're in the clear. Find the breach and move on."

Cameron shook her head. "We did find a breach, just didn't think anything of it. Joel swept the systems and found a hack into the CCTV systems after the attack started. Never considered for a moment that they've be looking for us. But how would they know where to hack – unless they've attacked every compromised business." She paused. "No, that doesn't make sense. Too many options, and anyway the breach occurred before the bank went public, I'm sure of it." She frowned, thinking hard.

Charlie was worried. He knew his little sister was dabbling in some dangerous networks. She was part of the thin green line at the forefront of the cyber security battle, and the foe was in the shadows. Organised crime? The remnants of hostile regimes? Nothing good.

"Play," ordered Charlie, and the broadcast resumed. The first picture faded and a second was displayed. "Hah, not to worry, there's another picture and it definitely isn't Ross this time. Colour shot, no ginger hair. Stab in the dark. You're in the clear, Cam."

Cameron looked up at him, feeling nauseous, suddenly pale. "No, Charlie. I'm not. Look at that picture again. Where are they?"

Charlie peered at the screen, and turned back to his sister, appalled.

"Oh, dear god, Cameron, that's outside your apartment."

She nodded silently, and her head swam.

•

Ross paced himself between splits, the monitor on his wrist counting down three minutes of recovery before his next four hundred metre sprint. He was sweating despite the cool morning, back on course with his training plan, but suffering from the interruption of the cyber attack. Two more weeks to the race, two more splits to finish today. Most of his training partners were already cooling down on the bikes, some pulling on compression leggings.

The monitor pinged and he accelerated, pushing himself hard as he pounded around the track. He should be faster than race pace. At the end of the lap, he spat in disgust at his time. One more to go, he thought, as he jogged slowly along.

Lucy whizzed past him in her racing chair, completing her final training lap. "Hey, Ross, smile, you grumpy sod."

He scowled, staying focused.

A passer-by leaned on the fence, watching him run. Ross took no notice, retreating into himself, drawing from a reserve of inner strength for the final lap.

He accelerated once more, pushing again as he rounded the first bend, and feeling released as his legs finally obeyed and carried him around the track to a strong finish. He punched the air and slowed to a jog, relieved. He followed Lucy towards the cooldown area next to a small stand that had been built along the straight, empty of spectators on a cloudy Sunday morning.

As he relieved his aching muscles on the static bike, the team coach approached him.

"Not bad, Ross, but you're cutting it fine for the race. I'm looking at final selections for the elite team next weekend, and there are some hungry youngsters snapping at your heels. I'm sorry to hear about your grandmother. I guess that couldn't be helped, but it really messed up the last week, didn't it? You need to pull something good out of the bag; you don't want to waste all that training."

Ross started guiltily. He needed to keep track of how many grandmothers' funerals he used as excuses to cover his increasingly erratic work commitments.

"Thanks, coach. She'd been ill for a while, but it's tough when they finally go. We've arranged the funeral so it doesn't clash with training."

The coach nodded sympathetically, and Ross felt like a fraud. Too many lies. He was starting to get out of his depth.

Ross headed for the showers, avoiding the rest of the team. His performance hadn't been up to scratch, and he knew they were all watching. The older ones, afraid he might let them down. The younger ones, sensing a chance for glory.

The Olympic selectors would be there at the race, putting the building blocks in place for Reykjavik 2048. Ross craved recognition; this might be his last shot as an amateur sportsman. He was anonymous despite all his efforts at work, and likely to remain anonymous despite all his sacrifices for training.

Boiling with frustration and anger, he stayed a long time under the cooling jets of water until the changing room fell silent.

Ginger hair still dark and damp from the shower, Ross walked out into the warming air. The door fell closed behind him, biometric locks securing the building until a registered club member came to open them again. He wasn't the last person to leave, though. Ross looked up as the club's groundsman rounded the corner.

"Hey, Ross, is the coach still around?"

"No, mate, you've missed him. Just locking up."

The groundsman looked crestfallen, and indicated the box he was carrying. "Ah bugger. This package just arrived for him. What am I going to do?"

Ross shrugged. "He won't be back until tomorrow. What've you got?"

"Dunno." He scanned the box. "Er, it looks like it's from the supplement suppliers. Yeah, here, look: 'Silent Running nutrition boost'. Hold on, it says it's been made up for you. There's stroke of luck. You may as well take it now."

"Thanks mate, I will," replied Ross, his mind racing.

The groundsman handed Ross the box, gave him a cheery smile, and waved as he returned to his work.

Ross stowed the box in his kit bag, pulled out his smartscreen, and switched it on. Within moments it lit up with alerts. Cameron. Ross connected a voice call as he strolled towards the station.

"Ross, I've been trying to reach you for hours." She sounded flustered. "Have you seen the public news channels?"

"No, of course not, I've been at training. What's wrong?"

"Someone's doxed us. The news has got hold of our

details and we're all over the headlines. Ross, they've got pictures, pictures of you at the bank."

Ross took a deep breath, trying to contain his excitement. Maybe, just maybe, his luck was turning. He fought to keep his voice light.

"Hey, Cameron, don't panic, it was going to happen one day, wasn't it? What have they said?"

"Ross, sod it, I am panicking, this is serious. There are some bad guys out there who may not be too happy about the work we do. They've picked up on my handle, but they've linked it with the team. They're saying you're me, which is pretty funny I suppose, but it potentially puts us all in danger."

He was taken aback by how concerned she was. Ross had never been convinced of her arguments about the dangers of their profession. There were probably thousands of people doing what they did. One threat intelligence group out of hundreds around the world. Okay, so Cameron – or her avatar, the SimCavalier – was well known; she'd cracked some big attacks, stopped them in their tracks, leaped to the solution with some fey intuition and no little skill. She deserved the public kudos. The whole team did. They'd be celebrities.

"Cameron, calm down. Most people in the business know the SimCavalier, same as they see me, RunningManTech, out there on the forums. Is it so bad to get some real publicity? I know you've always been hiding, but maybe it's time we were recognised for the work we do?"

Cameron took a deep breath at the other end of the call. She was furious. She needed to step back and deal with this professionally. Ross was a long-standing colleague and partner, but not a friend, she reminded herself.

"No, Ross. The position of this team is unchanged. We stay in the shadows. If you want to take advantage of this and move into the light, you do it alone. Your contract is very clear."

Ross kicked a pebble hard against the fence. It made a satisfying clang. Bugger Cameron and her obsession about secrecy. He said nothing.

Cameron paused. "Ross, they appear to have traced back to my home as well as hacking the bank cameras. We need a full investigation into the breach, and we have to close it down. Are you with me?"

That was a surprise. How the hell could anyone have found her home? Ross had thought even finding the right bank would be a long shot. They were dealing with hacks, not hackers.

"Yeah, of course I'm with you, Cameron, always," he lied.

"Team meeting, face to face, 10am tomorrow."

The call went dead. Ross scowled. It was going to be one hell of a meeting.

At the house, Cameron put the screen down, a knot of worry growing in her stomach. She realised that she no longer trusted her business partner. His reaction to the breach had changed everything.

•

The children were now up and in full voice, careering around the house with Roxy in happy pursuit. Tara was giggling hysterically as Nina caught her and tickled her under the arms. Dilan chased the girls, growling, in his dinosaur pyjamas. Cameron jumped aside to avoid being swept up in the tangle of children and dog as they crossed the upstairs landing. It was hard to be serious with this amount of laughter in the house, she reflected, grinning broadly. Today was her time; stop worrying.

Sameena came out of Dilan's bedroom carrying a pile of clothes. "Dilan Silvera," she called, "get your bedroom tidied! I have just found all your dirty school uniform under your bed. It needs washing for tomorrow. Go and put the rest of your things away."

Grumbling, Dilan turned away from the chase. "But Muuum…"

"Don't argue, young man, get organised. And you, Nina. Are you ready for school tomorrow? You have tests coming up. Make sure your room is tidy and you have everything you need. Tara, come and help me."

Cameron watched, impressed, as the children went about their chores. Sameena had them in hand, there was no doubt. She made a mental note to tidy her own room before she left.

"Sameena," she called, bounding down the stairs with Roxy, "I'm heading back to London this afternoon. Is there anything you need me to do?"

"So soon, Cameron? I had hoped you would stay until tomorrow morning. You are always welcome, you know.

And the children will be sorry not to spend more time with you."

Cameron was tempted to change her mind, but no, it would be a rush to get back if she stayed until the morning, and besides, she didn't want to break another date with Ben.

"I'm so sorry, Sameena, I promised a friend I would meet them tonight. I'll stay for lunch, of course, but I'll catch the train about four."

Mollified, Sameena smiled at her sister-in-law. "Vicky is coming for lunch. We will have some nice family time after all that fuss yesterday. Would Mandisa like to come over as well?"

"Great idea, Sameena," said Cameron happily. "I'll call her now."

•

The eight of them were crowded around the large table in the dining room. Nina was holding court at one end, with Dilan and Tara to either side of her. Sameena served the children from the large steaming bowls in the centre of the table, ignoring complaints of 'but I don't like onion'. Aunt Vicky, sitting between Sameena and Charlie at the other end, was in a much better mood.

"How's Donald?" asked Cameron, between mouthfuls of delectable chicken curry.

"Oh, he's much better, thank you, Cameron. I'm sure he'll be fine. He seems to have pulled round. He went out this morning and was back to his usual self. He dug up next door's bedding plants." Aunt Vicky sounded almost proud.

Cameron glanced at Mandisa, who was sitting next to her, and tried not to laugh.

"Was that next-door-Andrew-Taylor or the other neighbour, Aunt Vicky?"

"Oh no, not Andy. Henry, on the other side." A shadow passed across Aunt Vicky's face. "He doesn't much like Donald. And his dog keeps trying to get into my garden. The new wall makes no difference. Do you know, he wouldn't pay a penny towards it?" She paused as a thought struck her. "Oh, Cameron, Andy was asking after you this morning. He wanted to know about the training you do. I think his company in London wants to talk to you."

Cameron blinked. "Uh, okay, I don't turn down work… What's his business?"

"Oh, darling, no idea. Shall I give him your mailbox address?"

"Not the private one, Aunt Vicky. Ask him to contact Argentum – here, I'll write it down for you – and tell him I work for them."

Cameron exchanged a look with Mandisa. She was not happy about this at all. She changed the subject rapidly.

"Mandisa and I are thinking of a girls' week away. Get some sunshine. We've collected enough carbon offset credits for flights. Where shall we go?"

Aunt Vicky piped up, "We always went to Spain. Most of the big resorts in the south are under water but the northern coast is still lovely." She paused, and grinned naughtily. "Oh, we had such fun. The Canaries should be alright, surely, they have mountains?"

Charlie shook his head. "The weather there can be terrible. It's warm but it's wet. A last-minute trip when you know the weather forecast might work. How many flights do they have now?"

"Oh, not many these days," replied Mandisa. "The weather's caused problems for regular tourism and there are barely any scheduled flights. I'm thinking about the Emirates – they have a good flight quota because of their international trade and connecting routes, and it's just about cool enough at this time of year – it won't go over fifty. The hotels will still be open."

"That sounds like fun." Sameena's eyes were dancing. "Charlie, we should take the kids on a long-distance holiday. It would be lovely to fly again. We must be close to having enough carbon points for us all to travel?"

"Not far off," agreed Charlie. "Maybe next year? Let's start looking at what we could do. Shame most of the equatorial belt is out of bounds. Cam, do you remember going to Singapore with mum and dad when we were kids? The Gardens by the Bay? You must have been, what, eight?"

"Wow, yes, just. The photos are in the cloud somewhere. That was the last long-haul holiday we had all together." Cameron fell silent, remembering another time and place, another world, and the blissful ignorance of childhood.

Charlie coughed. "Anyone fancy a walk?"

The chatter picked up again as the children cleared the table and stacked the dishwasher, under protest. Roxy gambolled around, anticipating a trip round the fields. Aunt Vicky excused herself, but the six Silveras and Mandisa headed out along a footpath around the outskirts of the village. The clouds had started to clear, with patches of sunlight filtering through. The children and the dog jumped in puddles and squelched through mud, washing their boots and paws in the running water of the brook. Mandisa and Cameron strolled behind, at a precise safe distance calculated to keep them dry and free of mud.

"So, tell me more about this new squeeze?"

Cameron blushed. "Oh, he's just a guy I met at training. I liked him the moment I saw him, but he had a girlfriend. That was a while ago. Then he turns up, we're talking, I find out they've split up… The rest is history."

"Does he know what you do?"

"Not yet. Not exactly. Although I had to break a date last week, and then he came over on Thursday night and I got back so late that he must be wondering. It's not always a nine to five job."

"I need to meet him, Cam. I'm in the lab all of this week, but I'll be coming down to London for a conference the week after next. Drinks?"

Cameron gave in gracefully. "Of course. You can give him the third degree. You'll like him."

Mandisa smiled, victorious.

•

"The taxi's here." Dilan had been looking out for it. The tiny autocar pulled up in the entrance to the driveway and the door swung open invitingly. Cameron emerged from the front door of the house with Tara hanging onto her hand. "Aunty Cam, don't go."

"I'll be back soon. You behave yourself."

Nina sidled up to her. "Aunty Cam, can I do my homework in your attic? Please?"

The invasion begins, thought Cameron.

"Sure, babe. The computer won't switch on for you, though. You'll need your screen. And be careful with my things, won't you?" She treated Nina to a mock scowl, which Nina returned in kind. They glared at each other for a moment, and Nina cracked first, laughing. Cameron grinned and tousled her hair.

Charlie joined them, carrying Cameron's bag. "Be careful, little sis. We're here if you need any help at all. Let me know how you get on with Ross tomorrow."

Cameron nodded gratefully. The taxi beeped insistently.

"Better go – I don't want to miss my train." Bag stowed and seatbelt fastened, the autocar purred off up the hill. The roads were quiet, and Cameron reached the station without incident. As she boarded the train, her screen pinged, and a handsome face appeared: dark eyes, black hair, and a cheeky grin.

"Hey, you, I'm on my way home. Want to meet me at the station?"

Ben smiled, his eyes twinkling. "Sure. See you soon."

•

The last rays of the evening sun illuminated the terracotta tiling of the small restaurant, giving it a rich, Mediterranean glow. A waiter appeared at their table by the window, which looked out onto the street and a small city park beyond. There was more blossom on the cherry trees, and daffodils nodded in hosts on the grass, bright as dusk fell. "Would you like to see the dessert menu?"

Cameron looked up, glass of wine in hand.

Ben grinned broadly. "Always."

The waiter produced two small headsets, each with a clear glass viewer. They slipped them on, and gazed at the menu. Here, a tempting slice of chocolate fudge cake, icing glistening, whipped cream sliding slowly down the angle of the slice. There, a rich crème brulée, the caramelised top cracked, revealing the custard beneath. A portion of tiramisu in a tall glass, the layers of sponge, cream and chocolate moist with coffee and marsala. Lemon cheesecake sat on a plate, garnished with strawberries. Nutrition labels hovered over each choice, defining calories and sugar content.

Cameron pulled off her headset and the menu vanished. "Tiramisu, please."

Ben took one last, longing look at the delicious selection and handed his viewer back, too. "Crème brulée."

The order was in progress in the kitchen before the waiter turned away from the table.

Ben gazed outside at the light evening traffic as it flowed silently by. "Do you remember when we still had petrol engines?" he asked.

Cameron nodded. "Oh yes, I grew up a few miles from the race track. I remember the sound of the engines on Grand Prix day, those Formula One beasts, even at home in the garden. We had air force planes overhead from time to time, too. Although they still fly, of course."

Ben sighed. "My dad loved cars, and racing, and everything about them. He was devastated when the last of the petrol cars were forced off the road. We used to go to rallies. I drove, sometimes, I learned how to fix things – things the on-board computer didn't handle. In fact, some of the cars we worked on didn't even have computers."

There are still some old cars around, thought Cameron. Out in the countryside, where no one was looking. There were at least three such cars garaged in the village, that she knew of. Probably more.

Ben continued. "He goes to the electric Grand Prix, and it's exciting, but he says he misses the roar and the smell and the danger. I don't miss the pollution in the city, though." That was true enough. Respiratory disease was at an all-time low thanks to the clean air.

"Is that how you ended up in engineering?" Cameron was curious to know more about him. "What kind of things do you work on now?"

"I design for printers. It's all very well saying you can

print anything you want, but the blueprints have to be absolutely right in the first place. No use printing a bicycle that's missing a wheel, or makes the frame out of rubber and the tyres out of metal, is it." Ben laughed. "There are some terrible tales about that kind of mistake. A whole batch of whistles with no hole in the middle." Cameron giggled. "Chairs with three legs. Car doors with no handle or hinge." He shrugged, grinning. "Engineers have never gone away. We just changed the way we work."

Their food arrived, and Cameron took another slug of wine. She really didn't have room for pudding, but the augmented reality menu had been too good to resist. Ben tucked into his crème brulée with gusto. Cameron reckoned he'd be able to finish of the tiramisu if she struggled.

"So how did you get into tech, then?" he asked, as he scraped the last remnants of caramel cream from the side of the dish.

"My mum, I guess. She was always into computers. Bits of programming here and there, always up to date, made sure my brother and I knew the basics of coding and security right from primary school. I think I was six when I coded my first web page. It was very pink." She paused, reminiscing. "I was nine or ten when the first wave of big cyber attacks came. Lots of fuss about hidden 'bots, systems falling over, data breaches, people losing money through hard currency account scams and huge raids on the early cryptocurrency wallets. I remember thinking, surely this can be stopped. It's so easy to get it right, why do so many people get it wrong? That evolved into the work I do now. Training. Bringing people up to speed for their own good. Patching and fixing security systems. It's fun."

"Yeah, getting it right counts for everything," reflected Ben. "We're quite alike, aren't we?" He smiled at her, and her stomach did a backflip. "So that cyber attack, last week, is that why you had to break our date?"

Cameron dropped her gaze to the table. She really didn't want to involve Ben in the hidden part of her world, not just yet. "Yes. There were a few things to sort out. Don't worry about it. It's very rare."

The waiter approached and Cameron looked up, relieved at a chance to change the subject.

"Would you care for coffee?" he asked.

"No thanks," replied Cameron. "Can we get the bill?"

The waiter nodded and handed Cameron a screen. She approved the tab and tip, and thumbed a payment authority. The coins left her account instantly and credited the restaurant. The waiter smiled and retrieved his screen. "Thank you very much, you have a nice evening, now."

Ben gave two swift taps on the autocar call screen on the wall as they left the restaurant. A minute later, a small two-seater vehicle pulled up by the kerb. "Your carriage awaits, ma'am," joked Ben, executing a sweeping bow and guiding Cameron to the door. The taxi bore them back towards her apartment, and as Cameron settled in Ben's arms she was content. Cyber crime could just wait, tonight.

6: FOLLOW THE MONEY

Ben watched as Cameron gradually awoke, disturbed by the morning sun coming through the open blinds. She blinked her green eyes and they caught the light, clear and emerald bright. Ben smiled and gave her a playful poke in the ribs.

"Hey," she protested.

"Time to get up, sleepyhead. I have to get to work, and so do you."

Cameron yawned and looked around at the clock; Ben was right. She heard the faint sound of the cat mewing pathetically for attention, shut out of the bedroom. Cameron clambered out from an entanglement of covers and let the little animal in. She could hear the kettle automatically warming up in the kitchen, but coffee could wait for a few more moments. Snuggling back into bed with boyfriend on one side and purring cat on the other, Cameron was enjoying the calm before the storm.

Ben finally eased himself out of bed and walked towards the bathroom. Cameron heard the shower start to run. Spreading herself across the full width of the mattress without disturbing the cat, Cameron thought through the day ahead.

Team meeting. Sandeep, Ella and Pete had all seen the

news reports and had messaged her before she'd tried to contact them, absolutely raging. Susie didn't quite follow the extent of the crisis that had occurred. Still no word from Joel or Noor who'd both been out of connected range all weekend, but they'd get the message in time for the meeting. Cameron had no idea how it would go. Ross could be unpredictable and fiery, and his reaction to the broadcast images had been completely unexpected. She thought back through the time they'd worked together. Had he ever expressed this deep need for recognition? If that was really how he felt, he'd kept it very quiet.

Whatever the outcome, she would go the bank in the afternoon to work with Bill on planning training. The day to day work patrolling the borders of cyber security was her bread and butter, the life blood of the business she had built over the past decade. That said, the visit would be a good chance to dig deeper into the CCTV hack and try to get some leads.

She was fascinated by the message hidden in the Speakeasy subroutine. What did it mean? Where had the attack originated? Cameron quickly scanned the forums on her smartscreen. The community was still discussing its source and meaning, with no clear consensus. There were a lot of talented folk out there; between them, they could generally guarantee to take down, dissect, and trace the perpetrators of any attack in just a few days. There was a distinct feeling of frustration across the network that this mystery was foiling the best of them.

The best of them? Cameron knew she was at the top

of her game and commanded a lot of respect from her peers. It was no false modesty to say that she probably was the best they had, right now. They would be starting to look to her for answers. Time to get to work.

She sighed, and as the sound of running water ceased in the bathroom, she threw back the covers and stood up.

•

The offices of Argentum Associates lay behind a plain entrance in an anonymous side street a few hundred metres from Cameron's apartment. Sandeep was the first to arrive. He checked the coffee machine: supplies were running low. "Order a full set of coffee refills please, two litres of milk, and some fresh muffins."

"Order received, delivery in four minutes," replied a disembodied voice.

Sandeep opened the dishwasher and retrieved eight mugs which he placed on the table, along with a plate for the muffins. The delivery hatch beeped; he walked across to the wall and collected the order. The muffins were slightly squashed. Sandeep tapped the 'three out of five stars' option on the delivery hatch touchpad, muttering under his breath. He tipped the misshapen cakes onto the plate and looked up as Ella and Susie walked in.

"Good weekend?" Ella and Susie glanced fleetingly at each other, and Sandeep raised an eyebrow. "Really? Hah, you devils. Thought you were having fun on Friday."

Susie blushed. Ella deadpanned, and hurriedly changed

the subject. "Yeah, great thanks, until we saw the news report. What the hell happened?"

Sandeep sighed. "You know that second breach that Joel and I picked up while you lot were asleep on Wednesday? The hack into the CCTV? That's where some of the pictures came from. They had access to the live feed for around eight hours, maybe ten hours tops, but I wondered if they'd been into the archives. I guess this confirms the older records were compromised, after all."

Pete came through the door as Sandeep was speaking. "What I don't get," he said, "is why the hell were they in those records on that day in that bank? How did they know what they were looking for?"

"That's the million-coin question, isn't it, guys?" Cameron had arrived. She grabbed a mug from the table – another gift from the kids, with a cartoon dog on it – and placed it under the coffee dispenser. "Cappuccino." Turning away, she smiled as she saw the plate. "Muffins, good call. Where are the others?"

"Joel's running late, power outage on the Northern Line. I guess Ross'll be stuck in the same place unless he's cycling. Noor's on her way."

"Great, while we're waiting, let's have another look at that breach, Sandeep. Did you isolate the original trojan?"

"Yes, boss." Sandeep brought it up on the screen. "Very simple, dropped straight into the network past their two-factor authentication. Easy to identify the culprit, an employee on an unsecured wifi network outside the building."

Pete stepped up to the screen. "I've seen this style of code before. It's a real quick and dirty routine. Nothing sophisticated."

"Where have you come across it? We need some context, Pete. Sandeep, did you get details of where the employee was, what the circumstances were?"

"Sure, Cameron. Bill and I spoke to her. She went out for a break to check emails from her kids' school in the coffee shop over the road. That's a regular haunt of bank staff."

"City Coffee? I know it," interjected Susie. "In my last job, we did some work there, tightening up their access point. They were keen to be seen as a safe place for city staff to relax. I'd be surprised if anything got through. That was a year ago, but they're good with updates."

"Interesting. Sandeep, did you check the device? Smartscreen, was it?"

Sandeep shook his head. "Never thought."

"That's fine, it's been a busy week. I'm back there this afternoon to speak to Bill about training plans. Come along with me and do some digging." Cameron turned to Pete. "Where have you seen this before?"

"Not this exact thing, but the style's familiar. I think – and I could be wrong – it's old-school surveillance stuff. I'll run it by a couple of my contacts on the forums, see where it's popped up since military days."

The door opened and Ross marched in. "Sorry I'm late. Looks like there was a power outage on the tube. Bloody autocar swarm closed the road, couldn't even get through on the bike. Cleared now."

Cameron nodded. "Joel was stuck on the shuttle. I guess it's all recharged now, if the swarm has cleared." Sure enough, Cameron caught sight of Joel in the street view camera, approaching the door, closely followed by Noor. "I'm not convinced that commandeering autocars to recharge power failures is a great idea in the city. There'll be commuters and tourists stuck all over London wondering why their lift spat them out onto the street. More disruption than it's worth."

Ross laughed nervously. He hated the small talk. It was time to get down to business. "Yeah, it was a bit of a mess out there," he muttered.

All eight of them were now assembled, coffee and muffins in hand. No point delaying the main discussion. Cameron took on a serious tone. "Okay everyone." She took a deep breath. "You've all seen the footage that was broadcast on the news channels. How the team was compromised is something we will get to the bottom of later. Right now, we have to agree our position going forwards."

She paused, and looked around at her team.

"Your contracts all have a secrecy clause. I set up this business with my eyes open. We tackle the worst of cyber crime, we put up defences against perpetrators across the globe. We're not dealing with innocents. We're stopping not just idiots but determined criminals.

"Take your bit of sleuthing last week, Ella: you found

the spike in futures trading. We have a good estimate of how much money was creamed off the markets thanks to the Speakeasy attack. Ross, I see you put the details on the forums, thank you."

Ross looked shamefaced for a moment; he hadn't credited Ella with the find.

"Other teams have looked into the model and confirmed Ella's findings. Someone out there has made a decent profit, but it could have been a lot more. I bet they're not your average investor. It's very likely they commissioned the build of Speakeasy to create that artificial drop in value. I imagine they'll be a little pissed off that we stopped the attack in its tracks so quickly. What happens if they decide they need us out of the way so they can try again?"

Ross snorted. "I think you're blowing it out of all proportion, Cameron. This is central London, not the Rio favelas or the Macau underworld. You have more chance of being crushed by swarming autocars than being taken out by a Cosa Nostra hit man."

Cameron turned to him, face like thunder. "I hope you're right, Ross, for your sake, because it's your face that's plastered all over the internet, and your handle that's linked with the futures model."

Ross just glared at her, unable to respond.

Susie interjected. "I'm sorry, Cameron, I know we have the secrecy clause here, and I'm happy to abide by it, but we didn't have anything like that in my last job."

Pete shook his head. "Susie, you were out in the open

doing prevention work, brilliantly I might add. Now you're on the front line. It's different. It's more like the military intelligence environment that I used to work in. There are some dangerous people out there, and we're a hair's breadth from them."

Joel nodded in agreement. "I'm ex-army too, Susie. Pete's right. You can't underestimate the threat level." He looked at Cameron, and across to Ross. "I know they have Ross's face, so he's running the biggest risk, but they have your name too, boss. Judging by the other photos, they have an idea where you live, too. Who's the poor schmuck that looks like Ross, anyway? Do we have a responsibility to him? How do we protect you all?"

Cameron started to speak, but Ross cut her off. "What if I don't want protecting, Joel? What if, for once, for bloody once, we get some kudos from the public for saving their hides? For fuck's sake, Joel, you got a medal for sitting on your arse in a tent in the desert. We stop the whole banking system from crashing round our ears, the man in the street gets his pay credit and lives to spend another day, and not a whisper. The news channel's all over us because they want to thank us."

He was standing now, his face flushed with anger.

"Don't you see that? We're heroes. If we really are targets, hiding away puts us in more danger. Go public, and we'll get any protection we need, police, security, whatever." Ross slammed his hand against the wall in frustration. The monitor wobbled.

"Calm down, man." Sandeep put a hand on his shoulder. Ross shrugged it off angrily. The group was silent.

Noor spoke up tentatively. "I'm with Cameron. I don't want publicity. I just want to do my job."

Ross glared at her.

Ella rounded on him. "Ross, do you really understand what happened with those cryptocurrency futures? It looked like nothing much, a tiny blip, but it was a major manipulation of the markets. The timing had to be precise, the targets were carefully chosen – we're not dealing with amateurs. I don't know how we're going to do it now, but we have to protect our identities." She sat back in her chair, and glanced at Susie, who looked shell-shocked.

Cameron sighed. "Pete, Joel, I know your positions. Noor, Ella, thanks for your support."

Sandeep raised his hand. "I'm with you. Anonymity as far as the general public is concerned."

Susie looked at Cameron and nodded. "Me too."

Ross was shaking. "So, what now? You're out in the open, SimCavalier, 'I Cam Silvera'? Won't take them long to crack that, for all your stupid secrecy. 'I don't want publicity'," he mocked. "You've got it, what are you going to do?"

"They don't have me," replied Cameron icily. "They have you. Your face. My name, sure, but your face. They've done some real digging. Yes, they've photographed my apartment block, but they are looking for you. God help you if the wrong people find you first."

Joel looked at them both. "Ross, you're outnumbered

seven to one. No publicity. We can get our lawyers to force the images offline. Pete and I can tighten up security for both of you. God knows how they found your apartment, Cameron, I know how much you do to hide that address."

Ross grabbed his bag and headed for the door. "Fuck you, Joel, I'm not interested. I'll step into the light. I'm not afraid. I'll deflect them from Cameron though. How about credit for Speakeasy going to RunningManTech as far as the public's concerned? Make them forget the SimCavalier. You can stay in your hidey-hole."

The rest of the group sat, stunned, as he left the room, slamming the door behind him. They could hear him clattering down the stairs and out of the door.

Cameron felt sick to her stomach. She turned to Pete, and her voice shook. "Suspend all of Ross's access to Argentum Associates systems. We redouble our efforts to trace the breach back to source. We keep this team secure."

She leaned onto the table and put her head in her hands.

•

Bill met them at the bank's reception just after lunch. "Hi Cameron, good to see you." He shook her hand. "Sandeep, you too." Another handshake. He ushered them through the barriers and upstairs to the now-familiar meeting room. "Let's get the diaries on screen and organise these training sessions. How does next Tuesday look for you?

We can run four short sessions. That'll cover the bulk of the staff for a quick refresher. And Wednesday for a run-through with my team?"

"That's fine with me, Bill." Cameron reiterated the dates and times to her calendar. "You should get a confirmation through in a moment."

Bill's screen pinged. "Got it. That was easy enough. Anything else I can do for you now?"

Cameron looked him directly in the eyes. "We have another errand, I'm afraid. Did you see the news channels over the weekend?"

Bill nodded soberly. "Yes. That CCTV footage. Thank goodness you picked up on the breach at the time. Nasty stuff. What do you need from me?"

Sandeep spoke up. "We need to know more about the breach. We have to trace the source. Can I get a look at the device which was compromised? Do you have it?"

"Sure, the staff member concerned has been reprimanded but she's at work today. I'll get her in. Reception!"

The monitor came to life. "Yes, Bill?"

"Get me Tracy Gardner."

A momentary pause, and another face appeared on the screen. "Tracy, hi, can you bring Grace to the first-floor meeting room. Get her to bring her smartscreen with her." The face on the screen nodded assent and turned away to the bank of monitors behind her as the picture faded.

A few minutes later came a knock at the door. A nervous

looking woman in her early forties, small and overweight, was ushered in. She was clutching a smartscreen.

"Hi Grace, just sit down, nothing to worry about. You've met Sandeep Tahir before, and this is Cameron Silvera. You're not in any trouble, we just need a little more information from you."

The woman nodded nervously.

Cameron smiled at her, and spoke calmly. "We know it was an easy mistake to make, Grace. It's possible that someone went out of their way to trick you and you simply wouldn't have known. Well done for following all the security rules for authentication." Grace gave a cautious smile. "Sandeep here would like to have a look at your smartscreen, and I'd like you to tell me exactly what happened in that coffee shop."

Grace glanced at Bill, who nodded encouragingly. "Uh… I went out for my break early. I had a message from my kids' school. I've only just come back to work here, I'm normally working from home so I can sort things out straight away. Tracy let me go ten minutes before everyone else."

"Do you usually go there on break?"

Grace nodded. "Yes, a lot of us do, it's really handy and the cake's lovely. I've logged on in there before, loads of times, is that wrong? Everyone does it."

Bill backed her up. "Yes, I've done it myself. The café owner has always made a real effort to provide a secure environment, it helps trade. Bank policy is that two-factor authentication over a secure network is fine for remote access. How else would everyone work from home?"

Fair point, thought Cameron. But all the protocols and policies in the world could not secure systems against the lethal combination of determined hacking and human error. That was what paid her wages, and it would never end.

Sandeep looked up. "The café network is on there, properly secured from what I can see. It's been in regular use, but it wasn't accessed by this device on Wednesday morning."

Grace looked confused. "But… I picked the usual network and it connected straight away. They always change the password on Thursdays, and it was Wednesday, so I didn't even think."

"No, Grace, it picked up a signal alright, but not the secure café network. Look, here…" Sandeep turned the smartscreen around so everyone could see. "There's the café network, GreatCityCoffee, last access Friday, Thursday, Tuesday. You're certainly keeping them in business, aren't you. Wednesday morning, you were connected to this one – GraetCityCoffee. Looks almost the same. It would be the first to appear on an alphabetical list. If it was being generated within the café it may have been the strongest signal. It's completely unsecured so you'd go straight on."

Grace stared at him, wide eyed.

"You were unlucky, Grace. Whoever it was knew that staff spent their breaks in that café, and you were simply the first to arrive."

“Was there anyone else in there?” Cameron interjected. “Were you alone?”

“No one else was inside. I had the whole place to myself. Well, the waiter was there, obviously. There might have been someone at the tables on the pavement, I’m not sure.”

Sandeep looked at Cameron. “Would that have been close enough to generate a strong signal from a mobile relay?”

Cameron shrugged. “It’s our best guess. Go and pay them a visit. Get a feel for the distance the signal would have to travel. Grace, where exactly were you sitting?”

•

Sandeep stepped into the café. They were already cleaning up ready to close. The lunchtime rush had been over for an hour or so. A few chairs had been stacked on the tables. Sure enough, there in the far corner against the wall, furthest from the door, was the little sofa Grace had described.

The waiter glanced at him. “Can I help you?”

“Just an espresso, please.” The machine behind the counter flicked into life as water began to boil. The waiter lounged on a solitary chair, watching the news channel on a wall monitor, and glancing at both the coffee maker and the little vacuum ’bot that hummed around under the tables gathering up the crumbs and debris of the day.

Sandeep sat down on the sofa and stretched out casually,

gauging the distance to the other side of the café. It was a small space, and it wouldn't take a powerful relay to cover the whole area. But Grace had been alone in here. Could a signal get through the thick walls?

Looking closer, he noticed that part of the front wall had been knocked through at some time in its history. The inconspicuous partition that filled the void was designed to open, presumably to take advantage of the few days of English summer. This material was likely to be thin enough that a signal would not be obstructed. The theory was holding up.

His coffee arrived, a thick crema hiding potent dark liquid in the tiny cup. He drank it in one gulp, wincing at the caffeine hit. Good espresso, rich flavour, very smooth. Too many people confused bitterness for strength. He'd come back here, if he was passing.

Thumbing the payment, he nodded to the waiter and strolled back outside. Sure enough, there was a table set right next to the exterior of the partition wall. Any signal broadcast from there would deliver perfect coverage to the rest of the café.

Sandeep glanced around for cameras. There had been none in the café itself, but he spotted a familiar shiny globe on a lamp-post a few metres away. Public CCTV to the rescue. With luck, the last week's recordings would still be available, and Argentum Associates was one of the few private agencies who had official access to them.

•

Back at the office, Cameron logged on to the secure public CCTV archive. It wouldn't be hard to track the target. They had the location, and the time must be in a window of only a few hours. Sandeep's hands swept across the birds-eye view of London that was displayed on the screen, searching for the right camera, zooming down with precise little taps.

"Okay, there's the bank. Is that the café awning over the road? Yep. I see the tables. Ah! This is the one." Homing in on the camera position, the screen seamlessly changed to show the current view from the lens, and a timeline. Sandeep scrolled carefully along the timeline as the image flickered from light to dark and back, day and night. "Wednesday… 4pm, 2pm, noon, ten, eight… What time did the system breach occur?"

Cameron dug back into the files. "Uh… 10.32. Grace's office access record shows she went out for her break at 9.49. They worked fast, didn't they?"

Sandeep gently moved the images forwards, frame by frame. "The place is open… bit of a rush, must be breakfast time…" He counted the customers in, and counted them out again. "Okay, it's empty right now, that's 8.45am. Two, three, four people going in… two straight back out again with takeaway cups. Here's someone else… Sitting at the table nearest the door… Waiter comes out..." He kept scrolling. "9.25… two people leaving from indoors, they're the ones who arrived just before nine… Okay, another bod's arrived, sitting at the table next to the partition. Could be our mark. Waiter comes back, delivers to the new table. The person by the door's finished their breakfast… they've moved off… he clears the table… There. Nine fifty-two. Grace has arrived. So, the only other person at the café is this guy on the central table."

"Zoom in as far as you can," ordered Cameron.

"Can't get close enough to see in detail." Sandeep shook his head.

Cameron peered at the screen. Something about the figure looked familiar. It triggered the memory of a dog walker in the distance.

"You're not going to believe this," she said with mounting horror. "I think I know who that is. How the hell is he mixed up in this?"

Sandeep turned to her in surprise, but both of them were suddenly startled by an incoming call alert.

"Argentum Associates, can I help you?" Ella answered.

"Hi, I'm trying to reach Cameron Silvera," came a man's voice. "Is she available?"

Cameron waved frantically at Ella to stay off camera and keep the company logo on-screen, and shook her head violently.

"I'm sorry, she's with a client. May I say who called?"

"Sure," said the voice, jovial and friendly. "It's Andrew. Andrew Taylor."

•

Cameron returned to her apartment just after six, drained by the day's drama. She fed the cat and checked the fridge. Time to do some shopping. The discreet cylinder on the kitchen shelf relayed a list back to her, things she'd noted over the past week that had been used up. She added a couple of extra treats and placed her order.

Doing her shopping manually felt good. People tended to rely on their household tech to the extent they no longer noticed it. Her fridge did not do product promotion, or place orders automatically for direct drop to the shelves. For that matter, her portal was still an old model, sitting visible on the shelf, not integrated into the smart lightbulbs in every room. It wasn't the same as walking to a shop with a written list, but Cameron felt she was as much in control as she could be, without compromising comfort.

The cat skated through the apartment, its tail bushy with adrenaline. Drone on the balcony. Cameron opened the glass doors and collected her order from the little machine. To keep her hand in, and relieve some stress, she intended to cook. Fresh ingredients had come straight from the market stalls. She dug out her mother's old recipe book, heavily annotated, and searched for a skillet and saucepan, a chopping board, and a sharp knife. Most important of all, she picked a glass from the cupboard and opened a bottle of Yorkshire claret.

The sauce bubbling and pasta boiling, Cameron poured another glass of wine and turned to the computer. Gaming her IP address again, she logged in to the forums.

Most of the buzz was around the strange message they'd cracked on Friday, and the weekend's revelations on the news channel. She ignored the gossip around the news, other than posting a quick disclaimer to say that the pictures were not of her. No one on the forum knew her gender or location for sure; it would soon be written off as a hoax.

There was some activity around Ella's cryptocurrency futures analysis, posted by Ross. She frowned. He hadn't explicitly claimed the credit for that breakthrough, but neither had he given Ella, or the rest of the team, any mention. He was a funny creature. She wondered what he was up to. There had been no message since he stormed out of the office. Better to leave him be, leave him to train, get the fight out of his system. He'd either come back round, or the lawyers would silence him.

•

Ross eyed the encroaching storm clouds. Night was falling as he cycled home, and a chill wind heralded rain. He was still furious. Furious with Cameron and the rest of the team for their obsession with secrecy. Furious, if he dared admit it, with himself. He craved recognition, but always sabotaged his own efforts.

Two weeks before a big race, and he'd dropped his training to fix the cyber attack. Yes, it was his job, but deep inside he admitted that Cameron was a sympathetic boss, and would have made allowances for him, changed the shifts, accommodated his needs.

Ross pushed harder up Crouch Hill. His legs felt good. This wonder supplement could be helping to give him an edge. Of course, that could just be his imagination – these things took time to build up – but it was a nice gesture from the coach.

The rain began as he crested the hill, clattering on his helmet and soaking quickly through his jerkin. Sweeping into the estate, he stowed his bike safely and made it through the door as the storm hit.

Ross dripped his way to through to the bathroom and pulled off his wet clothes. He lay naked on his bed for a few minutes, staring at the ceiling, cooling gradually. Conscious that he was stiffening up, he made his way to the shower, enjoying the warmth of the water.

Clean and rested, he ordered the next meal in his nutrition pack. It dropped into the delivery hatch, hot from the kitchens, thirty minutes later. Protein and carbohydrates balanced to perfection, antioxidants boosting his immune system, and delicious too. Back on track. Only the race mattered now.

Supper over, glass of water in hand, Ross sat back and relaxed. He swiped idly at his smartscreen, and glanced at the forums, setting his status to Away, browsing and avoiding comment. He didn't want to talk to anyone. Posts full of bloody cats again. Honestly, they were supposed to be professionals. Cameron showed as active. Where did she claim to be posting from today? Tokyo? Hah. Total paranoia.

There was a flurry of activity on the thread around the hidden message. What the hell was 'hurricane season' anyway? Cameron would be in the middle of that, taking all the glory, no doubt. He had no wish to see her.

He glanced at the thread he'd started with Ella's theory on cryptocurrency futures. A few comments, curious to know more, but nothing had been posted for a while. They could wait. He logged off again, and loaded an old game. Lost in the challenge, making longer and longer links of coloured blocks, time passed quickly. When the alarm sounded for bed time, it startled him.

The lights of the main room faded with his footsteps as he trudged wearily to the bedroom. He still felt like a failure. For all his bluster this morning, he'd done nothing to make contact with the news channels. They were still searching in vain. Underneath his bravado, there was a tiny knot of worry. Perhaps Cameron was right, after all.

7: EXPOSURE

"'Batten down the hatches for hurricane season.' That's bizarre." Noor looked puzzled as Cameron demonstrated the cracked routine to the group.

"We know there's always another threat around the corner. Why bother to warn us? It's not specific enough to make any difference." Pete was equally confused.

"What's hurricane season?" asked Susie.

"The time of year when there used to be a lot of storms around the Caribbean," replied Cameron, reading from a wiki on the monitor. "Says here it used to run June through November, lots of big storms one after the other." She turned to Joel. "That's where your mum and dad came from, isn't it? Any insights?"

Joel leaned back in his chair and stared at the ceiling. "Haven't been back there for years. Still got cousins on the high ground. Not enough carbon credits for regular family visits. But yeah, hurricanes. Wow, there were some bad times when they made landfall. My dad was a kid when the big one hit the island. Ripped through the place. He and my aunts and uncles all ended up sleeping in one room in their grandparent's place, little more than a shack. That was before drones and 3D printers and shit. They had to rebuild the place themselves. That's why my dad left, in the end. Economic disaster. More jobs over here."

Sandeep chipped in. "They used to name them, didn't they, all the tropical storms?"

"Yeah, man, they're still doing it. There are just more small storms for longer, and then a couple of really big ones make landfall each year." Joel paused. "Don't you remember the big storm that hit Cayman last year? They called it Hurricane Usain, I don't think they'd been so far down the alphabet before. Wrecked the main financial district. All those offshore bank accounts were disrupted for days. Drone relief couldn't get through because of the winds. Took weeks to recover, and some of the last low-lying parts of the islands completely disappeared into the sea."

Sandeep and Ella nodded, recalling the news reports.

"Wow," said Susie. "Is it that bad every year?"

"Pretty much. If they're lucky, the storm blows itself out at sea, just some bad weather and waves. If it makes landfall – if it becomes a real hurricane - there's a lot of destruction. Nice analogy for a cyber attack. The attack hits its target, there's chaos. If not, if there's just a daft worm floating round, or a short-lived Distributed Denial of Service attack, there's much less disruption. We have to tackle both."

Sandeep turned to Cameron. "So, what does this all tell us? I guess the Speakeasy crew have other things in the pipeline."

"We know they can time attacks," Ella chipped in. "The

financial analysis showed the timing had to be precise for them to hit payday this time."

"If we work to the traditional 'hurricane season', June through November, I guess we have to assume there's something coming any time from a month from now to six months." Cameron shrugged, and Sandeep snorted with ironic laughter.

"Well, that really helps," he said sarcastically.

"Hold on though," said Joel, "hurricane season isn't one storm. This sounds more like they're throwing a whole bunch of things at us."

"Yeah, that's what we all thought last night on the forums," confirmed Cameron. "It won't change our normal defensive behaviour at all. If anything, we'll be advising our clients to tighten up. We stay right on top of updates. We put pressure on the software providers. We warn the powers that be. We'll have to, because if we don't, and an attack, or a series of attacks, happens, and they find out the whole threat intelligence community sat on their hands, didn't react to a warning, there will be hell to pay."

"Damned if we do, and damned if we don't." Joel frowned.

"I don't get it," said Ella, flatly. "What's in it for them? If we close them down, if we're watching for the next attacks, then won't they lose out?"

"Vanity?" suggested Pete. "Mad cyber criminal, James Bond style, telling us the plan because they're sure we won't live to tell the tale?"

Cameron shook her head. "I don't know what's going on here, but I do know we have absolutely no choice but to redouble defensive efforts." She gathered her thoughts. Time to make a start. "Noor, can you analyse the last, say, fifty years of hurricane records and see if there's a pattern, a peak? That may give us a better feel for the timing of a major attack. Sandeep, Susie, check through client records, see if we can bring forward security reviews, highlight any sensitive systems."

Ella interjected. "What about that enquiry yesterday? Andrew Taylor? He was asking about training."

Cameron scowled. "I don't know what he wants, but I'm willing to bet it's not training."

She glanced at Sandeep and raised an eyebrow. They had kept their findings quiet until now; it was time to share them with the team. "I met him at Charlie's this weekend. There is a chance that he has something to do with the CCTV breach. I don't know if this call is pure coincidence and a genuine enquiry, or he's put two and two together and linked Argentum with the pictures." She paused, considering her options. "Tell you what, Joel, Pete, can you pick this one up? Get a feel for the situation. Find out where he's coming from. We'll take the business if it's genuine, of course, otherwise scare him off if need be. Keep me out of it for now."

The two men nodded, and went into the small alcove reserved for training calls, careful to position the camera so that the other party would see only the two men, and the company's logo on the wall behind.

Cameron called over to them. "I messaged Ross on Saturday to dig around and find out about him, but he never came back to me. Not enough data, I guess. But here's what I know already." She flipped his name, address, and description over to their screen.

"Cheers, Cameron. We're on it."

"Ella, can you go back to your cryptocurrency futures. If that's the best way for the Speakeasy crew to make money, can you model some likely scenarios for profit? We can keep an eye on the markets and possibly steal a march on them."

Ella smiled, and bent to her work. Cameron knew where the strengths of her team lay. She also knew she was missing Ross, for all his moods and fury. He might change his mind. She hoped so.

•

Andy abandoned the London office in favour of home. They'd had no contact from the mysterious SimCavalier, nor from the anonymous source of the tipoff that had led him to the bank. His attempts to speak to Cameron had met with a brick wall. Two brick walls, to be precise.

"Mr Taylor? My name is Joel Bardouille, this is my colleague Peter Iveson. We've received your enquiry about a cyber security review and training."

Even on the screen, Andy could tell these were big lads.

"If we can run over a few details about the business,

and we can arrange a site visit to discuss in more detail. What's the company name?"

Andy panicked slightly, and obfuscated as best he could. "Oh… it's not my business, I'm enquiring for a friend. It's just that I met Cameron, Cameron Silvera, at a social event and she said she did training…?"

"That's correct, Mr Taylor," replied the bald man, Peter. "I'm afraid Ms Silvera is occupied on another contract. Would you like us to contact your friend directly?"

"Uh, no, I mean, uh, I can take details for now. He has, uh, a manufacturing business. Just a small operation. What kind of things do you offer?"

"The standard service, Mr Taylor," Joel explained smoothly. "We conduct penetration tests on the network and servers, identify any weakness that may be vulnerable to direct attack, review your friend's software for the most recent security updates, and deliver staff training. It's normally human error that compromises any installation."

Not much different to my job, thought Andy. Human weakness brings in the stories. He reflected on the tipoff he'd received. What weakness had prompted that exposure?

Odd, though. Cameron had said she worked in robotics training. Had these two gorillas gotten the wrong end of the stick? Or was she closer to the world of the SimCavalier than he'd anticipated? Was her presence at the apartment block no coincidence?

"So, I guess Cameron would handle the training? Could I possibly have a chat with her when she's available? I'm sure we can arrange the other things with my friend, but I would love to find out about…"

"I'm sorry, Mr Taylor, but Cameron is completely committed for the next few weeks with existing contracts and a planned vacation. I am sure that Joel and I will be able to complete whatever is required. It's not something that should be left for long."

Andy admitted defeat gracefully. "That's fine, thank you, gentlemen. I will speak to my friend and come back to you with his answer." He terminated the call, puzzling over the new twist.

At the other end, Joel and Pete, sat back and laughed. "Round one to us, Cameron. He didn't know where to look. He's determined to get to you, isn't he?"

"Find out who he is, will you? Aunt Vicky was clueless. She thinks he's great. I don't reckon there's anything sinister going on with him, but he may be mixed up in something bigger. It really doesn't feel right."

Sitting in his study at home, looking out towards the village street, Andy reflected on the call. Although he was no closer to Cameron herself, he knew she had lied about her work. She was concealing something. Protecting a boyfriend? Time to do some digging with his neighbour.

Andy brightened up as he heard a drone arriving. One of the big advantages of living in the country was the access to fresh food straight from the farms round about. As the world warmed, the supply grew of local fruit and vegetables that once had to be imported. He stood up and went to the front door to collect the delivery.

The drone slowed, approaching its destination. At that moment, a ginger streak flew out of the bushes in his neighbour's garden. Jumping and twisting in the air, Donald brought the drone down, skilfully dodging its rotor. Andy howled with rage, watching his fresh avocados bounce down the hill. Donald sat, purring loudly, one paw on the crippled machine as it struggled weakly to fly.

Aunt Vicky rushed out of her house, as fast as her legs could carry her. "Donald! Donald! Bad cat! Bad!" She flapped at him ineffectively with her hands. He ignored her, and rolled over, toying with his catch.

Andy had a better idea. Whistling for Jasper, the dog came bounding out and Donald took fright, belting back into the bushes at high speed. Andy picked up the remaining produce, and pressed the breakdown button on the drone. Within the hour a recovery drone would arrive to pick up its fallen fellow and bear it away for repair.

Aunt Vicky wrung her hands and stumbled out an apology. "Andy, I'm so sorry, naughty Donald, he hasn't been well, you know."

"He looks perfectly healthy to me, Vicky." Andy softened. Here was a golden opportunity. "I was about to put the kettle on. Care to join me?"

•

Cameron and her team settled down to the familiar routine of contract work, the Speakeasy threat averted and the ripples of that initial disruption fading. With the hurricane warning uncovered, and a man down on the team, there was more urgency to their delivery. Ross had sent a curt message asking for two weeks off to focus on his race. Cameron granted it instantly.

"Hey, Noor, how's that pen test going? Want a coffee?" Ella looked over at her colleague, hard at work digging through the servers of a small insurance group.

"Love one, thanks Ella. This system is like a sieve. It took me less than an hour to get through. The developers should be shot. I've managed to get hold of some of their stored hashes, I've dropped some scripts into the existing code and they haven't been pushed back, and the session information is wide open. Going to be fun tightening it all up." Noor smiled, satisfied at a job well done.

"Wow, that's bad. So, if you were up to no good, you could identify data in their blockchain, drop a mine in there to collect information whenever you wanted it, and keep an eye on who's accessing the system? Nasty."

The door opened, and Sandeep and Joel appeared. "Coffee time? Perfect."

"How did the training go, guys?" asked Ella. "You were over at the university today, yeah?"

"Oh wow," sighed Joel. "They may be the brains of the country, but some of them really haven't a clue about cyber security. The amount of legacy software they hang on to is appalling. The IT guys know their stuff, but they're fighting a losing battle. The academics have settled into a nice routine of teaching the same thing year after year, so they keep an old device with a defunct operating system to run their out of date materials, then they hook it up to the network, and the whole place is wide open. No clue."

Sandeep grinned. "Joel was pretty surprised. I've seen it before. They're all wrapped up in their own worlds. Takes a lot of careful nudges from us to bring them up to speed. We're getting there, though. Managed to prize an old Windows 20 laptop off someone today, their IT girl said she owes me, she's been trying for years."

Cameron, Pete and Susie trooped in, returning from a patch-and-update job. "Bang up to date. All finished." Cameron turned to the accounts controller. "Complete signoff for SussexGrid and issue invoice."

A disembodied voice replied. "Invoice transmitted. Can I help you with anything else?"

"No, that's all for now." Cameron turned to the rest of the team. "Hey, I'm meeting some friends later, want to join us for a drink? I know it's a school night, but we're doing well. We've earned a break."

They gathered at a big table in the window of the busy pub. Pete tapped out their orders on his smartscreen and they thumbed their individual payments over to his account. A few minutes later, the drinks were delivered to their table.

"No drones?" asked Susie.

The waiter laughed. "The wooden beams play havoc. Kept catching the rotors. Beer showers for the punters. Much easier to deliver by hand."

"Cheers." Pete raised his pint to his colleagues and Cameron's friends.

"Introductions," said Cameron, taking a drink. "Most of you know Mandisa. Mandisa, this is Susie, she's just started with us. And this is Ben." No further details. Joel raised an eyebrow discreetly at Ella, who grinned, guessing that this must be the mysterious boyfriend.

Pete glanced over at the monitor on the wall, showing the latest news. "Hey, guys, the latest Mars mission is taking off. Look – live shots from Kazakhstan."

Ben spoke up. "I got involved with this, a bit anyway. Engineering for the 3D printers they're taking. They literally have to print all the tools and equipment they need. Much easier to take a hold full of extruded raw materials ready for the printer than the actual items, especially if they have to deal with unexpected situations on-planet. It's sustainable, too. They can recycle and reprint."

The others around the table looked impressed.

"Wow, that's really something," said Noor. "You're part of the expansion of the galactic empire."

Ben laughed, embarrassed. "I guess so. In a really small way. Amazing though, that printing was the breakthrough for colonisation. Who knew?"

Mandisa grinned at Cameron. "I like him," she whispered. "If he can hold his own with this crew, he's a keeper. Are you bringing him on holiday?"

Cameron shook her head, and whispered back. "Not enough flight credits, and anyway, it's our break."

Ben spotted them conspiring together, and smiled

affectionately across at Cameron. She grinned back, smitten. Mandisa could be right.

•

Race day arrived, grey and damp. Ross rose with the murky dawn just after five, and made his way to the start to meet the team. Race pack full of energy gels, invigorated by a strong ten days of training, he proudly pulled on the elite team colours.

The coach gave him a slap on the back. "Brilliant work the last couple of weeks, Ross. You've really focused, and it's paid off. You're in the shape of your life."

"Couldn't have done it without your support. I appreciate you going the extra mile for me."

The coach gave him a curious look. "All your own work, Ross. Now, go and show them what you're made of."

Ross adjusted his wetsuit and made his way to the pontoon on the north side of the lake, poised to dive into the chill waters of the Serpentine. He could see the bikes lined up in the distance, ready for the second leg. He held his nerves steady, and bumped fists with his team-mates. They were ready to go. The whistle sounded, and he dived, thinking of nothing else but his race, focused completely on his task.

•

"Bloody hell, Ross, you knocked it out of the park!" "Well done, mate, fantastic race!" "Knew you had it in you, you grumpy sod."

Ross couldn't control the grin that spread across his face. Personal best time, in front of the Olympic selectors. Right up there as part of the elite team, keeping the youngsters at bay.

The coach arrived, congratulating all his athletes. "You've all come on massively. That was a hell of a performance all round. Some brilliant personal best times. Dave, Adebayo, Ross, Tomasz, top class showing for the elite today. I'm proud of you all."

Ross was happier than he'd been for months. The exercise high and the buzz of recognition coursed through his veins. This was what he wanted, this was worth the sacrifices.

Maybe walking away from Cameron had been the key to focusing on his training. Had he overreacted? Perhaps. It would be time to take stock next week. He still hadn't followed up the news channel broadcasts. With nothing to add to their first revelation, the story had faded. He was old news.

Was it time to offer an olive branch, try to regain Cameron's trust? Once the celebrations were over, he'd think about it.

He and his team-mates were borne off to cool down and collect their gear. Tomasz and Dave drew the short straw for post-match testing along with the placed competitors, and disappeared to the officials' tent. Ross slowly packed up his wetsuit and bike, changing back into his regular grey hoodie. The cheers were still ringing in his ears. Most of the spectators had now drifted away, although one middle-aged, balding man still stood by the finish line, his unblinking gaze focused on the athletes as they as they left the park.

•

Andy was getting frustrated. It was more than two weeks since the pictures broke, and he hadn't had a sniff of the real identity of the SimCavalier. The forums he prowled under an anonymous handle were silent; the subject had been discussed, rebutted and dropped. The SimCavalier himself had posted a clear statement that the pictures were not of him. Andy suspected this was purely a smokescreen.

He needed Cameron to join the dots, but she would not respond to his calls. The muscle from her company, the two ex-forces lads, had made it very clear that she was unavailable, unless this was a genuine sales enquiry. His appeals to Aunt Vicky seemed to have fallen on deaf ears – she was more concerned about that awful cat, and although after Donald's attack on the drone she had promised to speak to her niece, nothing had come of it.

"No choice, Giles. Let's go and pick him up. I don't want to tip my hand to Cameron, it'll get me into too much trouble at home. Total discretion, okay?"

Giles laughed. "Aunt Vicky sounds formidable."

They walked towards the cluster of autocars that sat waiting outside the office block, nose-in to their charging stations like a row of multi-coloured suckling piglets.

Andy winced. "Oh yes. She keeps me in order. She keeps most of the village in order. Her cat's another matter. Furry bloody liability."

"How are we going to do this?"

"Can't risk Cameron spotting me, if she's there, so we'll keep away from the apartment itself. If you play the lost tourist, get him to the car, I'll be waiting. Just want to confirm his ID, see if he wants to play ball. If so we bring him in."

A large blue autocar detached itself from the cluster and rolled silently to a stop at the kerb. "Borough Underground Station," Giles ordered. The car waited for their seatbelts to click, and pulled off towards the main road. "Looked like he was heading that way the morning we photographed him. With luck, we'll pick him up on the way home."

Positioning himself outside a busy chain café, midway between the station and the turn to the apartment, Giles sipped coffee and water and scanned the passers-by for his mark. Mothers with pushchairs crowded the café and pavement tables, meeting friends for a chat and a break before collecting older children from school. Looking up for a moment, Giles saw heavy-laden delivery drones flying along the street high above the silent traffic. Sunlight glinted off solar panels, some static, others jutting from the rooflines, turning constantly to catch the rays as the sun moved across the sky.

He re-focused on the swelling commuter crowd coming from the direction of the station, and after almost an hour he spotted the distinctive grey hoodie. Thank goodness it was another cool day.

Leaving his seat, to the delight of the mums who immediately took over his table, he hurried further down the road and crossed over, perfectly timing his walk to intercept the man. Digging his smartscreen out of his pocket, he unrolled it and brought up a tourist map, pretending to study it as he struggled against the flow. He bumped artfully into the man in the grey hoodie, and dropped the screen. The man stopped and apologised.

"No problem, pal, my fault. Hey, do you know how to get to the market?" He pointed vaguely at the map, and the man frowned.

"You're going completely the wrong way. Here, follow me."

They set off northwards, Giles thanking the stranger profusely.

A few blocks later, the man paused. "I'm going this way, you just carry straight on, you can't miss it."

Giles thanked him again, and made to walk off. He could see Andy out of the corner of his eye approaching his mark on the side street. Andy drew the stranger aside and out of view. Neatly done, thought Giles.

He turned back and listened, out of sight. The man's voice was protesting, confused. "I don't know what you're talking about. My name's Rory MacPherson, I'm a researcher, I work at City University, I'm doing politics." He pulled out an ID card, and Andy studied it.

"Could you tell me where you were on Thursday 13th April?"

"Yes. I was at the university all day. Conference for external students. Presented a paper in the morning. There's footage on the university site."

Andy blinked. It was a cast-iron alibi. There was no way this could be the SimCavalier; no way he'd have been in the bank that day to be caught by the CCTV. He'd been over and over those pictures for two weeks, and he'd known all along that something didn't feel right.

He had the wrong man.

"I'm so sorry, Rory. This appears to be a case of mistaken identity," he said smoothly, handing back the ID card. "Please accept my apologies for bothering you."

Andy walked off up the main road, catching Giles before he was seen. Rory stared after him, shook his head, and walked on towards his apartment.

Andy slammed his fist against the wall in frustration. "The wrong guy. It's not him. I'm as sure as I can be that the SimCavalier lives right here. Maybe the guy on the bank footage isn't our man either. What have we missed? Let's get back to the office."

•

The two of them pored over the stolen CCTV images, frame by frame.

"Here's our man arriving on his own. Yes, I see now, the logo on his sweatshirt is a different shape, larger. Rory's in the clear. I knew there was something wrong. How did we not pick that up?"

Giles ignored him. Frustration and hindsight were not going to help. "There's another group coming in, but there's a glitch in the recording – look, it jumps, just there. Can't see much."

"Hmmm." Andy paused the playback and peered at the screen from every angle. "One tall guy with dreadlocks. That's odd, now, he looks familiar. I'm sure that's the muscle from Argentum. Joel Bardouille. Almost definite." There was a cold feeling in the pit of his stomach.

"Short dark-haired girl."

"Big solid bloke with no hair." Andy was sweating now. That could be other guy who'd been obstructing him for the last two weeks. Had he accidentally stumbled on the right group through Cameron?

"I can't make any of the rest out… Fast forward. Didn't we pick the original guy leaving around eight the next morning?"

Giles scrolled through the footage quickly, swiping the time bar sideways until he reached the morning. There was an influx of people running jerkily through the hall as the recording speeded forwards. Giles stopped it quickly. "Yeah, here we go, battling against the flow, our man with what looks like the same short dark-haired girl."

"And here they come back. Breakfast run. Okay, what was our next sighting?"

"Lunchtime. That was the last time we picked him up on camera before the feed was closed down. Look… here he goes. The dark-haired girl too. Your big bald guy, wouldn't argue with him. What about those two? The girls? Blondie in a short skirt, dark girl in trousers."

"Possibly. Yes, look, they've caught up with the other three in this next shot."

"So far so good," said Andy, still mystified. "So, there's five of them. Did you pick up any of the other guys over at the apartments? Mind you," he laughed, "could be one of the girls. You never know."

Giles shook his head. "Definitely not seen them before. The girls don't look…" Andy sat forward suddenly, cutting him off.

"Hold on. Where's the guy with the dreadlocks. He didn't leave with the others."

Giles turned back to the screen and scrolled through slowly. "Nothing yet… Ah, there. On his way out. There's three of them."

Andy took one look, and put his head in his hands.

"Oh god. It's her. It's Cameron. She's the one. She's our SimCavalier."

•

Ross slept late. When he woke, he was still on a high from the race. He dressed quickly and left the house, ignoring the chatter of the coffee machine. Making his way to a favourite café, he looked forward to the rare treat of eating a forbidden pastry and watching the world go by.

Sitting on a stool at the window, he watched idly as people passed by on the narrow street. Colleagues on their way to work, chattering in twos and threes, exchanging tales about the weekend. Solitary figures listening through earbuds to their personal soundtrack for a Monday morning, or focused on their smartscreens. Some were quite unaware of their surroundings, moving on autopilot. Others were scanning the world around them through an augmented reality lens, on screen or built into glasses, picking up advertising and offers from stores as they passed.

Music played in the café, and a monitor showed the news channels, presenters mouthing silently. Ross ignored both. Flipping through the latest news on his smartphone, watching occasional videos of the race, he didn't notice the stranger until he sat on a stool beside him.

"Good morning, Ross."

Ross started and looked round, confused. A fan? Where had he seen him before?

"You had a good race yesterday. Congratulations. Lucky you weren't picked up for testing, isn't it?"

The truth slowly dawned. "I don't know what you're talking about. I'm clean."

The man shook his head sadly. "Oh Ross, 'Silent Running' supplements? Did you really think your coach had ordered those for you?"

Ross's mouth went dry. "But… but… they came from the usual place…?"

"You understood what you wanted to believe. You took the help that was offered. You achieved your goal. As did I. RunningManTech, my employers would like your help. And you are in no position to refuse."

8: SALVAGED HONOUR

Ross's world came crashing down around him. He could feel his heart thumping in his chest. He looked at the stranger in horror. How could he have been so stupid?

"Come with me."

Ross stumbled out of the café. The man guided him to an autocar that waited nearby. "Get in."

They travelled in silence for almost an hour.

The autocar stopped in the middle of an anonymous industrial park in the suburbs. Blank office windows reflected the light. A small grove of wind turbines whirled in the light breeze. Every building had a south-facing pitch with solar tiling, drawing energy for the workers below. A few patches of scraggy grass attested to attempts to landscape the park, but they had fallen into neglect.

The stranger led Ross, still stunned and unresisting, through secure doors to a featureless, cream-tiled lobby. He gestured to a windowless office off the hall, which held a monitor, two chairs, and a table. Ross sat down heavily on the thin fabric cushion of the furthest chair, and leaned on the table, his head in his hands. The stranger took the seat nearest the door, demonstrably blocking Ross's exit.

The monitor on the wall hummed into life, a camera

lens waking above the screen. Ross looked up, but the screen, though lit, stayed blank. Ross had no doubt that the camera, on the other hand, was actively broadcasting his reactions to the party on the other end of this call.

"Good morning, RunningManTech." The voice was synthesised. Could it be an artificial intelligence? Ross suspected not; this was simply a way of remaining anonymous and hidden.

"We have been following your career with interest. Unlike others in your field, you make no attempt to hide yourself."

Ross blinked. This had to be a joke. They were playing a trick on him, taking the mick over his attitude to privacy.

The voice continued. "The insights you have published show a comprehensive grasp of the mechanics of cyber manipulation. However, your most recent postings touch on the motivation of agencies like ourselves. We are concerned."

Ross found his voice. "Guys? Is that you? What the fuck are you doing?"

"This is not a joke, RunningManTech."

He knew that. The sting was serious. There was no way his workmates could be involved.

"Okay, I'll play along for now," replied Ross with false bravado, trying to keep the tremble from his voice. "How do you know who I am?"

"As I say, you make no attempt to hide. We have been following the activities of all leading threat intelligence specialists for many years. One by one, they have hidden themselves away. They conceal themselves behind anonymous nicknames. They mask their locations. They know we are watching. You, however, can be easily traced. From your home to your club to the businesses in which you operate, your location is always known. As you posture and brag online, you act as if you are immune."

Ross licked his dry lips. "So you know about RunningManTech in cyberspace. Who's to say that's me? Check the news channels. Seen the pictures two weeks ago? They say I'm the SimCavalier. You sure you got the right man?"

"Yes. Those reports are a distraction. We have known you for a long time." Images appeared on the screen: Ross at his home, last summer, in the garden. Ross with training partners at his running club, wrapped in a tracksuit, in winter. Ross and Cameron leaving the bank together, probably when they finished the recent job.

"We have a job for you, and you cannot refuse our request. You know that your sporting career depends upon it."

Ross put his head in his hands. He felt sick. What the hell had his hubris dropped him into?

The voice continued. "First, you recently posted your theory that the Speakeasy creators profited from the manipulation of cyptocurrency. Have you shared this theory elsewhere?"

"No." Warning bells were clanging, too late. He had to hold back from revealing the team's involvement, and the detail of Ella's work, for which he had claimed credit on the forum.

"Good. We have suspended new posts to that thread, reducing interest and speculation. We will resume these online discussions and provide our own proofs to discredit your findings. You will confirm that your analysis was inaccurate, and that your claims were pure speculation."

"Yes," said Ross quietly.

"Second, we are aware that you have close connections with the specialist known as the SimCavalier. We require you to update us on all his progress and insights as our next wave of attacks is deployed. If he becomes aware that you are working for us, it will be more than your sporting career that suffers. Do you understand?"

Ross stared in horror. The room swam around him as he tried to stand. The stranger at the door pushed him back into his seat.

"Your tacit agreement is not required." The monitor clicked off, and Ross allowed the stranger to guide him outside. He stopped and vomited violently onto the patch of thin grass by the door. The stranger waited until he had finished, then unceremoniously pushed him into the autocar, and it glided away.

•

Another hazy day in the desert, sand masking the blue sky. Mandisa shrieked with delight as the vintage land cruiser crested another tall dune, her stomach leaping as they swept down a near-impossible gradient. The line of preserved, petrol-powered 4x4s snaked across the undulating sand, each driver carefully following the tracks of the leader and throwing up a localised sandstorm in their wake. In the distance, the sun glinted off an expanse of solar farms. Closer at hand, they could see more solar panels on a stationary roof, the only clue to their destination. Tourists from Dubai and Abu Dhabi were taking an adrenaline-fuelled journey towards this shining star in the east, eager for the 'authentic Bedouin experience', buffet barbecue, and belly dancers.

Mandisa glanced across the seat at Cameron. "Isn't this cool? Best way to get you to relax."

Cameron flashed a broad grin, green eyes masked by designer sunglasses, clinging to the armrest on the door as they were flung around like riders on a rollercoaster.

The passengers in the two seats behind them looked less comfortable. These old vehicles running on fossil fuel were a novelty, but the smell of exhaust fumes and the noise of the engine, coupled with the violent movement, was making the other occupants look rather green.

To the relief of their companions, the land cruiser slowed to a halt, parking up with the rest of the fleet, disgorging gaggles of tourists at the camp. Several rushed for the toilets, others climbed a nearby dune, sliding down on makeshift sledges. Camels were tethered close by for short rides, once stomachs were settled from the drive.

Mandisa and Cameron climbed the dune, feet slipping as they struggled to gain purchase in the sand. Reaching the crest triumphantly, they gazed to the west as the sun dipped towards the horizon.

"Great to be off-grid for a few days, huh?" Mandisa looked sidelong at her friend.

Cameron grinned. "I'll still be checking the net when we get back to the hotel, but yes, it's a novelty alright. Anyway, the team has everything under control. Nothing urgent. No problems that they can't deal with."

True seclusion was getting difficult to find in an ever-more connected world. Some corners of the north of England and the Scottish Highlands had kept their dark skies and deliberate no-coverage stance. National Parks across the world were also, as a rule, havens of peace.

Gazing at the endless expanse of dunes and solar farms that stretched into the distance, Mandisa sighed with pleasure. She missed the warmth and big skies of her native South Africa, even though she had only returned to visit her grandparents a handful of times since emigrating at the age of eleven. This rare trip to the desert seemed to be a suitable panacea.

There was a general movement towards the compound as the sun finally set, and the evening's entertainment began: food, drink, and dancing. They tucked into barbecued meat and salads, seated on low cushions around the stage, relaxing in the desert warmth as the dancers performed traditional routines in flowing, cool costumes. Even in early May, the evening temperature was close to thirty degrees Celsius. No wonder the summers were now too hot for tourists.

The darkness around the compound had become total, and the entertainment ended. The host called for quiet, and one by one the lights in the compound dimmed. Lying flat on their cushions, Cameron and Mandisa's eyes adjusted to the blackness, and they stared at the myriad stars which revealed themselves. There were gasps around them. Dark skies were a rare treat.

"Where's Mars?" whispered Mandisa under her breath.

"It's really faint at the moment," Cameron answered quietly, careful not to disturb others who lay in silent awe. "It's coming back from its furthest point from Earth. There… I think it's there… see the red dot? It doesn't twinkle like the stars."

"I see it… so the mission is on its way to intercept it at its closest. That's neat. Hey, do you think we could see the rocket?"

Cameron laughed softly. "Hardly. It's more than a week out, it'll have passed the moon by now and be on its way."

There was a hum of low voices around the compound as people pointed out constellations, planets, and distant galaxies to each other.

"Just imagine," reflected Cameron, thinking of her boyfriend and wishing he had been able to come with them, "Ben's 3D printer programs are on board. I wonder what the first thing they'll print will be?"

"A bottle opener, no question, celebrate the landing." Mandisa giggled, then groaned and squinted as the lights began to glow again. The evening was at an end. They got up slowly and reluctantly gathered their belongings.

joining the other tourists who were shuffling towards the parked land cruisers for the return trip.

The journey back was much shorter and smoother. The theatre of crossing the dunes like adventurers seeking a remote oasis masked the fact that there was a perfectly serviceable metalled road close to the compound, which ran straight back to town. Climbing out of the archaic vehicle at the door of the hotel, Cameron gazed up at the curved flanks of the majestic building, LEDs bathing it in ever-changing coloured light. The window of their room looked down on the old race track, the hotel forming a bridge. There were still cyclists training, or simply having fun, under floodlights in the relative cool of the night. She thought about Ben and the high-octane Formula One races of years ago. It must have been spectacular here when those races were running, engines howling and echoing under the hotel bridge as the drivers battled for position. Electric races were as fast, but the visceral thrill of the sheer noise had gone.

The next morning, the two girls discussed plans for their final couple of days over a leisurely breakfast.

"We could go to the waterpark again," suggested Mandisa. "Loads of fun, and it's going to be a hot day."

"Could go this afternoon… I fancy a trip into town, do some sightseeing. We haven't really left the island yet, apart from the desert trip."

Settled on their plans, the two of them hailed an autocar at the door to take them to downtown. The road swept past the huge development at Masdar, planned as the world's first zero-carbon city. Abandoned for years, it now had a new lease of life as renewable power generation technology caught up with the dream. After all, the country which had been built on the riches from fossil fuel now had to rely on the sun for its wealth, and it was succeeding against popular resistance, gradually winning round its people.

Passing the splendid white domes and minarets of the Grand Mosque, Cameron was surprised to see crowds. A demonstration? There was a sense of anger and noise, and more autocars were arriving from all directions. What could have sparked such a gathering? Mandisa shrugged; there had been nothing on the news channels.

Onwards to the downtown area, and the air of menace still hung around them. Cameron started to see posters in Arabic plastered on walls and on ad screens. Raising her smartscreen, the translation subtitles appeared. "Modesty for women!" "Bring back the hijab!"

Cameron frowned at Mandisa. "This is strange. Why would that argument be rearing its head again? It's years since the change, even here."

Mandisa was equally taken aback. "I don't like it. Something feels wrong. Let's just go back to the island... I'm not comfortable."

Cameron nodded. They took the cowards' way out, returning to their safe tourist haven and forgetting the troubles of their hosts as they squealed and screamed their way down flumes and slides like children in the bright sunshine.

The next day, sadly, they took their leave of the hotel, and made their way back to the nearby airport. Here, too, there was trouble.

"Fuel is not just for planes!" translated her smartscreen. "Fuel is our right!"

The two women skirted the protest and made it into the departure hall, crowded despite the handful of flights that were scheduled. The queue moved slowly, and Mandisa anxiously checked the time. "I don't understand the delay – we're cutting it fine."

Sure enough, a harassed-looking staff member came up and down the line. "Passengers for London? Passengers for London? Straight through here please."

They were ushered to a new desk to check their credentials and luggage. "I'm sorry ma'am, I can't retrieve your booking." Cameron glowered at the desk clerk and presented her screen with all the details on it. The poor man poked ineffectively at the keyboard, glancing at his colleagues who were all struggling too. "I will have to label manually… here is your reference… please proceed to the border controls."

"I smell a cyber attack," whispered Cameron to Mandisa. "I want to get home. I'll have a look at the forums when I get the chance."

Border control was no better. Where systems had become increasingly smooth over the years, easing from paper passports and rubber stamps to distributed, verified credentials held in the identity blockchain, there were border police milling around in confusion.

"Looks like they can't access the blockchain from here. Everyone is having to present verification manually, and that takes forever. I haven't seen this level of chaos close up for years."

"At least they're holding the flight," Mandisa pointed at the departure listings. "We'll be on it."

Curled up at the departure gate with her smartscreen, Cameron navigated quickly to the forums. A login from the Emirates wouldn't give her away. She'd used this location as a mask before; it should be lost in the noise. "Hey guys, what's going down?"

"Hey SimCavalier, good to see you. You've been quiet recently."

"Busy, guys, don't think I've been ignoring you on purpose. Need to know about any reports of compromised systems in the aviation sector and across the credentialing blockchain. Acting on a tipoff from a friend." She raised her eyebrows at Mandisa, who grinned.

Another member chipped in. "Reported glitches in credentialing, nothing major, the blockchain isn't compromised but there's been a DDoS attack on some key servers."

A distributed denial of service attack? Interesting, thought Cameron. That was an easy way to cause a lot of disruption, preventing normal queries from the border staff but without accessing or damaging the data.

"Several airlines are reporting failures in flight

administration systems," came a second contributor, "but not across the board. Low level stuff, generally where updates haven't been applied."

"Thanks everyone. Catch you later." Cameron turned to Mandisa. "Nothing major. Some security loopholes being exploited, and a DDoS attack. It'll all be back online before we get home. More updates to do."

Boarding had finally started. Cameron and Mandisa took their seats for the long flight back to London.

•

Andrew Taylor had a lot on his mind. Once he had joined the dots between Cameron and the SimCavalier, he was lost for what to do next. His journalistic instincts cried out for the story. His basic human decency – rare in the profession – was pushing to protect her. She was Charlie's sister. Vicky's niece. She had battled to protect her identity for years, certainly for longer than he had been pursuing the story. Could he bring himself to compromise that for his own short-term glory? He suspected he'd be chased out of the village with flaming brands and pitchforks – or worse, with Donald on his tail.

Decency prevailed.

Andy tried calling her office again. Feigning continued interest in their services from the fictional manufacturing business, he enquired after Cameron. Away on holiday, he was told.

He approached Aunt Vicky. She was in a sulk after Boris

had won a significant battle against Donald to reclaim control of the roof of the garden shed. Stop bothering my niece. She's too young for you.

Finally, Andy had no choice. He went to see Charlie.

Sameena opened the front door with a welcoming smile. "Charlie should be back soon. He's collecting Nina from swimming club. Come on in, Andy."

She showed him into the family room, where Dilan was working on the computer. As his mother came in, he started.

She looked at the screen and sighed. "Dilan, you said you were doing your homework. That is a game. Have you finished your maths?"

"Yes, mum. I promise. Can I keep playing?"

"Hmm, okay, but now Andy is here you should log out. Go and play outside. It's a nice day."

Andy laughed. "I was the same at his age. Let me think, what did we always slope off to play? Minecraft, was it? Yes, that's right. Great fun."

Sameena shook her head. "I couldn't get into that. My brothers enjoyed it, though. You should compare notes with Charlie on Minecraft, he and Nasser are always laughing about something called 'Stampy Longnose'. Ah, here he comes now." She went back into the hall. "Charlie, Andy is here. Shall I make some coffee?"

Charlie came in, jovial and relaxed. "Coffee sounds like a plan. Nina, go and hang out your swimming kit. Hi, Andy. What's up? Did Sameena mention Minecraft just then? Don't tell me you played that too?"

"A bit," replied Andy, relieved at the small talk. "I was a teenager when it came out. Great way to relax when I should have been doing homework."

Sameena reappeared with coffees, as Charlie reached over to an old bookshelf, dusty and untouched for years. "Hey, have a look at this. My Official Construction Handbook. I was, what, ten when I got this. Rollercoasters and diamond fortresses and pixelated pigs. Loved it."

His wife laughed as she left the room.

Andy swallowed. "Look, Charlie, I'm sorry. I need to talk to you about Cameron."

Charlie looked intently at him, suddenly concerned.

"No, nothing bad, at least… It's complicated. I've been trying to reach her. I need to talk to her. It's to do with my work. And hers. I need your help."

"What do you mean?" asked Charlie, puzzled. "Researching? Interviews? What interest does the news-watching public have in robotics training?"

Andy couldn't meet his eyes. "I'm sorry, Charlie. I know that's not what she does. I've been following the SimCavalier for years, detailed investigative work, trying to find what I thought was the man behind all this great security stuff. I even had a tipoff about the last cyber attack. I had no idea…"

"Jesus, Andy…" Charlie looked stunned as the pieces clicked into place. "Don't tell me those news reports last month came from you?"

Andy nodded miserably. "We thought we had him.

Then I met Cameron here in the village. I knew I'd seen her before somewhere. It took me a long time to put two and two together." He grinned weakly at Charlie. "She's bloody brilliant, you know. A real superhero. She's saved the country's bacon more than a few times. Nothing but respect for her in the industry."

Deep down, Charlie was raging, furious that the sister he still unconsciously protected had been so close to exposure and danger. He couldn't really blame Andy, though; this was his job, and it was pure chance that Cameron had fallen into the path of his investigations.

"She won't talk to you. She won't step out of the shadows. It's too dangerous. Didn't the possible repercussions ever occur to you? Why do you think she was so hard for you to track down?"

"I know. I've told my editor we've lost the SimCavalier for now, that the tipoff was a hoax, and I'm still looking. I couldn't do it to her – to you – to Vicky." Andy looked across at Charlie. "I'd like her to work with me. If I can deliver cyber security scoops, it'll be a payoff for the years of research, keep my editor happy. I give you my solemn word that I won't compromise her identity."

Charlie looked thoughtful. "I can't speak for her, but I'll call her. She's away, due back this evening. I can't promise how she'll react, but thanks for coming clean. I appreciate it."

The two men stood up, and Andy shook Charlie's hand firmly. "Thanks Charlie. I'm sorry. I'll see you later at the pub?"

Charlie gave him a genuine smile. “You will. Thanks, Andy.”

•

The first day back in the office is always stressful, Cameron reminded herself, as she settled back into the daily routine. A couple of smaller payments remained outstanding from clients: that was rare. Most contracts now triggered a coin transfer as soon as completion was confirmed by all parties. Debt collection was a job for Sandeep at his most persuasive. The human accountant at the other end of their AI interface reported steady cashflow, all salaries paid, and sales performing to target. It was a good time to be in the cyber security business. Cameron smiled wryly. She and her peers were probably the most consistent beneficiaries of cyber crime over time. The thought made her pause: park that intuition for another time.

Noor gave her a summary of news over the last week. “We’re starting to see updates coming through from major software suppliers for the weaknesses that were identified through Speakeasy. I’ve done an initial review of all our clients and we’re booking them in for visits, tests and training. There’ve been a lot of new enquiries through, too. It’ll be good to have Ross back.”

Cameron looked up quizzically. “He’s been in touch?”

“Oh yes, he asked for a meeting with Pete, Ella and the lawyers. He’s very contrite. He says he completely understands the concern over privacy, he's taken no action over the news reports, and he would like to come back to work."

That was good news, thought Cameron. For all his moods, he was thorough and worked hard.

"Great, I'll check things through with the legal team and get him back in the office. Looks like we have a busy summer ahead. He'll have plenty to keep him occupied."

She was still scrolling through reports when a call alert came through on her private screen. Charlie.

"Hey Charlie, what's up?"

"Hey Cam, couldn't get hold of you last night. Good holiday?"

"Fantastic, back in harness now though. Flight was delayed so we got back pretty late." She giggled. "Cyber attack on the airport systems. How ironic."

"Cam, I've been talking to Andy Taylor. No – wait," he continued hurriedly, as Cameron glared at him. "You need to hear this."

"Charlie, I know he's your friend, but…"

"Cam, listen. Do you know what he does?"

"No. He's been telling people he works with some manufacturing company, wanted training, I don't believe him."

"Oh shit, okay, I should have told you weeks ago but it didn't seem important. He's a journalist."

Cameron gasped in shock. "What? I didn't see that coming. Why the hell didn't you tell me, Charlie? You know the score."

"I know, I didn't realise he'd been trying to speak to you. He's been talking to Aunt Vicky too, but it never occurred to her to mention it. But Cam, it's okay."

Cameron snorted in derision.

"Let me finish," insisted Charlie. "He's made the connection between you and your public handle. He's been working on the story for years. As soon as he realised it was you, he pulled the plug. He wants to talk to you, but he won't expose you. I trust him. Why don't you meet? You could come here?"

"Too busy to come up right now, but I'll think about a meeting. Do you know what he wants?"

"I think so. He's looking for a story, of course, but what if you worked together? Give him some good cyber tales to write about?"

"Keep your enemies close."

"That's the spirit, Cam. So, shall I pass a message back to Andy? And what about this mystery boyfriend? Mandisa seems to think a lot of him."

•

Cameron arrived early on the terrace outside a bustling café by the river. She picked a table on the fringes, conscious that she wanted an easy exit. Joel lounged on a chair few metres away, browsing on his smartscreen. He raised it slightly, squinted, and laughed. Cameron caught sight of the logo of the latest craze in augmented reality games. She wondered what mythical beast he'd spotted floating down the Thames.

A cleaner 'bot arrived, all arms, and quickly tidied the debris of the last customers' refreshments onto a tray, before rolling away to the kitchen. A human waiter appeared and took her order; the café chain prided itself on these personal touches.

As the girl turned away, a voice called out. "And an Americano, please." Andy slid into the seat opposite Cameron.

She looked daggers at him.

He had the grace to look embarrassed. "I'm sorry."

Cameron sighed. "You're sorry that it was me, or you're sorry for trying to expose a completely innocent party to potential danger and end their career?"

"I'm sorry it was you. I knew the consequences of the investigation could be difficult, but I was following the story." He looked rueful. "Ethics and consequences are not always at the forefront of news gathering."

"You're right there." Cameron laughed despite herself. "So, where do we go from here?"

"I gave my word to Charlie, we are not running the story. My editor is furious with me, thinks I've given up, and so close to the prize. I'd love to put someone on a pedestal to recognise the work you do, even if it can't be you. Who was the guy we filmed, anyway?"

"Oh, he'd lap up the attention, he would. But he wouldn't have a job any more. Strict secrecy clauses. No hero for you, unless he goes out on his own, and he wouldn't last five minutes." She paused. "Okay, you don't have a story. What do you want from me?"

Andy leaned forward, keen to get her on side.

"Okay, there are plenty of good tech journalists following the scene, sources who help out when there are attacks, that sort of thing. I'd like you to be my source. Get the real story out there from a top threat intelligence operative – heavily disguised, of course."

"Dark glasses and a false nose, that'll do it."

Andy grinned.

Cameron looked thoughtful. "There's a lot of daft stuff gets written. It could be good to have a public voice that doesn't compromise our position."

This was looking promising. Andy ploughed on. "This could be a partnership, Cameron. I bet there are things we work on that could help you do your job. Stories that come to us, advance warnings, news that hasn't broken. We had an anonymous tipoff that you would be in the City of London during Speakeasy – would it have helped you to know about that?"

"So that's how you found us. Interesting. You moved pretty quickly."

Andy blinked, startled.

Cameron laughed at his confusion. "We did our own investigations, Andy. Why do you think I've been avoiding you? Saw you bugging the café that Thursday morning. We didn't have to hack anything to find you, either. Sloppy."

Andy gave her a sideways look and she grinned at him.

"I guess we'd better alert the bank they've got a mole. What time did you get word?"

Andy thought for a moment. "Late on the Wednesday afternoon. Took us a while to figure out where exactly we were looking. Had to narrow it down through reports of outages."

"That early, huh. That's pretty much when the attack started. The leak must be high up."

"Actually," replied Andy, "we can't be sure that it came from the bank. In fact, as it specifically mentioned the SimCavalier, I'm certain it's originated from the cyber security community. Could that be the case?"

It was Cameron's turn to be wrong-footed. "That never occurred to me, Andy. Not something I'd expect from our side." She paused, reflecting. "Andy, I accept your apology, and I trust Charlie's judgement. I think we can work together. I'll help you with good stories, you help me with an eye on the wider world."

"Thank you, Cameron." Andy was enormously relieved. "Look, there is one other guy at work who knows who you are. My colleague Giles. He's been with me on this story. I'd like to bring him into my confidence. Don't want him accidentally blowing your cover. Is that okay with you?"

Cameron nodded. "Yes, as long as you can trust him. You know that if he causes any trouble, the deal is off, and Charlie will know about it."

Andy winced. "It's your Aunt Vicky who scares me more, Cameron. I would hate to cross her."

He looked up as Joel wandered over in response to a wave from Cameron. "Andy, Joel, I know you've met before." The two men shook hands. "We're going to do some work together. I'll brief the team this afternoon." She turned to Andy. "Let's set up a more formal meeting, get your man Giles in too, and see exactly where we can help each other." Cameron drained the last of her coffee and stood up. "Better get back to work. Thanks, Andy. See you soon."

Andy watched the two of them as they left the terrace, and waved as they turned the corner. Relieved, light-headed, he felt as if a weight had been lifted from his shoulders. He had played fair by Charlie and Vicky, and salvaged his own career.

9: HURRICANE SEASON

Ross looked downright miserable as he sat facing his colleagues in the Argentum Associates office. Cameron had cleared his return with the lawyers, and his access to the company's systems had been restored. Nevertheless, he felt as if he was on probation. In the back of his mind, he tried to suppress the horror he felt at the betrayal he was undertaking. It's the only way, he reminded himself. The only way to keep his reputation as an athlete intact. Possibly the only way to stay alive. He was under no illusions that the stranger and his associates were deadly serious.

"Nice to see you, Ross," ventured Susie. "How are you doing?"

"Great run in the qualifiers," said Sandeep encouragingly. "That's you with a shot at the next Olympics, is that right?" He sounded impressed.

"Good to see you got down to some solid training when you had the chance," added Joel. "Cleared your head, yeah?"

"Thanks, guys. Yes, it was a good race." Ross's voice was flat, despite trying to sound pleased. A good race, perhaps, but at such a price.

"I'm glad to be back," he continued. "I'm sorry. I misjudged the mood around publicity. I didn't mean to fly off the handle like that. The whole fuss has died down, anyway. No more news reports."

"Cheer up, you grumpy sod. It's water under the bridge now." Cameron continued, brisk and business like. "You need to hit the ground running, RunningManTech. We have a lot of work to do."

"'Batten down the hatches for hurricane season.' Yes, I guess we do. What do you want me to cover?"

Cameron pulled up a work schedule on the nearest monitor.

"We've got some patching and updates to do for a raft of clients. New security updates have been released by some of the major software providers for internal server operating systems and the big utilities installations. Standard stuff. Noor, Sandeep, Pete, Joel, can you make sure they are applied across the board."

The four of them nodded. "Sure, Cameron, in hand."

"Ella, can you and Susie keep digging on those financial models." Cameron paused. "Ross, you know you dropped some info about the futures trading scam onto the forums? I notice that there's been a bit of activity there recently, and the work has been widely discredited. Even you chipped in on the thread to say you're not sure it's genuine after all. What's going on?"

Ella, startled, protested. "What the hell? Those figures are good…"

Ross started to apologise. "Ella. I know your work's sound. I'm sorry, but I thought it would be better to downplay the findings."

Ella had a face like thunder.

Ross rushed on. "Isn't it a good thing, though, with this focus on secrecy and everything? Not playing our hand publicly? I thought it would help."

Cameron shrugged. "Forums are hardly public. We need other teams to know what they might be facing. Ella, keep working. We'll publish insights as we go along, and keep our banking contacts informed."

Ella looked happier.

"Okay, Ross, I need your analytical brain. Work with the others client by client, get into any old, patched, custom systems, chase down the vulnerabilities that you find. Sweep for phishing emails. I'll handle the ID 10-T factor. Identify obsolete software that really should have been replaced. Refresher training across the board, try and minimise human error. Ella, Susie, when you're not crunching numbers you can get involved with the training too."

There was a flurry of movement as the eight of them got up from the table and moved to separate screens around the walls of the office. The level of noise rose as calls were placed to clients, appointments booked, and plans made. Cameron glanced across at Ross, who was coding up a scanning routine for deployment in email servers. He looked pale and drawn, but was absorbed in his task. He should be happy, she reflected. He'd been desperate to return to work, and he'd posted a fantastic time in his last race. Everything should be coming up roses. What could be bothering him?

Ah well, that was Ross. She dismissed the thought, and went back to her work.

•

It began slowly. The powers in the shadows gently teased the public networks, their untraceable 'bots provoking arguments, fuelling divisions, and spreading falsehoods across vulnerable communities. Uncorroborated statements and provocative posts were shared and spread like wildfire, as people shared whatever accorded with their world view, disregarding evidence and experts. Sources went unverified as memes and fake news gathered millions of followers, polarising communities and stirring up conflict.

Andy was the first to notice the trend as he monitored post sentiment across the world.

"This is odd," he called over to Giles. "Have you seen the latest global mood scores?"

Giles looked up, and a few other heads appeared over their monitors. There was a hum in the newsroom. "What's going on, Andy?"

Casting the graphs to the big screen, Andy explained. "This is a live feed tracking the moods of posts on all the public communities on the web. The tone of posts, the content, the frequency, the use of language; all together these indicate whether people are happy with what's occurring in their lives."

"Clever stuff," observed Giles, impressed.

"Oh yes. We keep tabs on moods. It's very interesting around election time, gives us a heads-up on national reaction to political statements during campaigns. Some governments are finally getting wise to tracking sentiment around policy statements, too."

Giles nodded. "I remember seeing these when we covered the presidential election two years ago. No one expected Bruno Mars to clinch the nomination; we spotted it before it happened."

Andy grinned. "Yeah, that was a good one. We've been staying right up to date with these stats ever since. Never know what we'll pick up next. So, the last couple of years in the US have been generally pretty stable. There's always discrepancy between rural and city mood ratings depending on policy emphasis but it's not too abrasive. We see a nice sweep of polarised moods country-wide around Superbowl time, but that's all good-naturcd stuff, to be honest.

"In England and Wales it's the same picture, generally. You get the occasional blip with big sporting events. Scotland depends on the time of year: happier when the days are longer. Weather patterns have an impact on mood, which is always a laugh but hindsight's no use in that business; the weather channel scoops us every time." There was a ripple of laughter round the room.

"Europe, steady patterns of happiness, occasional sweep of common misery as against pockets of delight when the extreme right wing are agitating. Russian bloc, still assimilating the re-absorbed nations and sketchy connectivity, but moving around a steady average."

"What about the southern hemisphere?" called an Australian reporter from the other side of the office.

"Southern hemisphere? You're all mad as a box of frogs. Says so here."

"No change there, then," chuckled the heckler.

"Moving on…" Andy grinned. "Latin America and Africa are really diverse but mood patterns hold regardless of individual national cultures. Asia, now, that's a tough one. China's a nightmare to track. So many different platforms; we get some decent data from Renren, Weibo and Fenda but it's not enough to draw inferences…"

Giles interrupted. "Okay Andy, we get the point. You know your way round these trends, and they're normally pretty steady within their own cultures and political systems. So, what's going on?"

"Unfounded polarisation is what's going on, Giles. Have a look at the last week for – what's this first one – Europe. Okay, we've had steady fluctuations as we'd anticipate for most of the year. There've been no significant policy announcements or major incidents. No sporting events on a national scale. But look: over the last month we've seen greater extremes of happiness and dissatisfaction."

Giles nodded. "I see that. Are you sure there's no local variation around, I dunno, weather, like you say, or kids being off school. That'll affect the happiness rating for parents." There were a few knowing laughs from their colleagues. Andy shook his head.

"No, we've adjusted for those. Some of the trends are actually reversing the expected social mood for the time. Bank holiday in the UK, no rain, everyone's grumpy. Where's the sense in that?"

"Fair point," Giles nodded. "What about the others?"

"Here's the US stats. You can see the big blip for the Superbowl back in January. Then everything settles back to where it should be. Now, all of a sudden: boom. Polarising sentiment. No reason for it.

"Look at England and Wales again: there's a blip around the local elections in May, and the FA Cup Final, but those have settled, and to be honest there were no real surprises." He flipped quickly through the remaining pages. "They're all the same. Something's going down and we don't know what it is. Fortunately, I know someone who will." He grinned at Giles. "Let's go and see our friend."

•

Cameron was alone in the office when the entrance alert buzzed. Glancing up at the screen, she saw Andy and Giles hovering on the street. "Let them in," she ordered, and then watched as Giles followed Andy out of street view and onto the hallway cameras.

"Morning, Cameron. How are you?"

Cameron shrugged. "All the usual stuff, Andy. Training idiots to change their passwords and remember them, and reminding them not to trust email clickbait.

Patching systems that haven't been updated because there were more important things to do. Gently teasing obsolete software out of the hands of people who are convinced they don't need an upgrade. Same old stuff." She looked up and smiled wryly. "What can I do for you?"

"I've got a puzzle for you to solve," declared Andy. He yawned suddenly.

Cameron glanced at him. "Late night? Get yourselves a coffee." She nodded at the machine in the corner.

Andy looked grateful and barked, "Americano. Double," in its general direction. He laughed. "That bloody cat of your aunt's, Donald, was scrapping all night. Wrestling with the noisy black cat over the road. I ended up chucking a bucket of water over them. That soon shut them up."

Andy collected his coffee and sat down opposite Cameron. He gestured for Giles to join them, and brought out his screen. "Okay. Cut to the chase, we're seeing some bizarre polarisation of opinion and sentiment worldwide. We don't know where it's coming from. We think you might."

Cameron nodded approvingly. "Good. I think I have an idea. I started noticing this when Mandisa and I were on holiday. The country's stable despite all the changes over the last decade, but there was something kicking off under the surface. Demonstrations at the airport against the aviation exclusivity on fossil fuel. Protests in the city calling for the return of the hijab for women. As you say, polarisation. I got Noor to have a detailed look at the local web activity, as her Arabic is way better than mine, and she identified an increased output of downright inflammatory stuff from sources that are almost certainly chatbots."

Giles leaned forwards. "What do you mean?"

"Okay," said Cameron. "Chatbot 101. At any time, at least a fifth of the accounts across web communities are not human. We've known that for more than twenty years and we still can't find a way to stop it. They just keep springing up. Most of the time they just tick over, automatically spewing whatever poisonous viewpoint they've been programmed to reflect."

Giles raised his eyebrows. "That many? Really?"

Cameron looked at him. "Check your own accounts. Do you know everyone you talk to? Do you know the source of everything you read and share?"

Giles thought for a moment, blushed, and shook his head. Cameron continued. "From time to time, we get a spike in chatbot activity which can directly influence human behaviour. We saw this back in 2016 with elections that took place at the time. In societies where closed communities formed online, chatbots reinforced consensus reality, created online echo chambers, and polarised public opinion."

Giles was looking confused again. "Consensus reality? Echo chambers?"

"Honestly, Giles. You must have come across this. Where everyone in your group thinks the same, so you believe the whole world works like that? Call yourself a journalist… jeez."

Andy jumped to Giles' defence. "He's too young to remember all of that. I'm surprised you remember it yourself, Cameron."

She laughed. "I remember it, all right. It's what first got me interested in this whole area. Apparently, these polarisation strategies, helped by a fair bit of malicious hacking and some seriously biased news reporting…" Cameron gave Andy a mock scowl. "They worked okay in Britain and the US where there were large online communities reinforcing each other's opinions, but were picked up when the French didn't play ball. Not so much reliance on those online communities, so less of an echo chamber for extremism. Different cultures, you see."

Andy nodded. "I see. But if that kind of thing only worked in certain cultures, what's behind this new spike?"

"Well, the world has moved on, we're more reliant on the web than ever, so the influence will be greater. If it really is impacting worldwide, then from what Noor found in her research, the provocation is very specifically targeted to prey on different national sensitivities. Let's have a look at the kind of things that have been trending."

Andy pulled up the first set of results. "Unites States. What've we got? Uh… okay, there's a bunch of stuff on gun law, calls to repeal the 2029 automatic weapons ban. Anti-vaccination propaganda, going after the ovarian cancer vaccine this time, blaming it for every birth defect they can think of. And some fossil fuel activists, same as you saw in the Emirates. They're always ranting on somewhere, but right now there's a real flurry of activity."

Giles was working through the files. "Here's another one, some agitation in Spain against foreign pensioners using all the healthcare resources." He laughed in disbelief. "That's crazy, it's their disposable income that's keeping the economy afloat since cheap holiday flights ended. Oh, and there's also a wave of protests from Catalan nationalists over the resettlement of refugees from the south."

Cameron was listening intently. This was going far further then she'd suspected. "Looks like there's some fairly sophisticated manipulation going on. I wonder, what's the rationale? Any indication of who's behind it?"

"As far as I can see," replied Andy, "there's no obvious regime leader looking smug out there, everyone's been affected to some degree. There are no significant elections coming up. Who's going to benefit?"

"That's the key, isn't it? Follow the money." They were all silent for a moment. "I'm going to get Ella to run some models. I wonder how this could impact on the markets?"

"Do you think this is significant, then?" asked Andy. "Has it started?"

"I think so. We may be into hurricane season."

•

Pete and his buddy checked each other's scuba equipment and prepared themselves to jump off the small boat as it bobbed, out of sight of land, over the site of an old shipwreck. “Ready?” “Ready.”

Pete jumped first, holding his mask and valves tight to his face. His fins hit the water, spread one in the front of the other, slowing his entry into the chilly sea. He felt the pressure of water on his body as he dipped briefly under the surface, then emerged again, buoyant. He could feel cold water penetrating his neoprene gloves and hood, trickling across his hairless scalp, although his body stayed dry, the suit sealed tightly at his wrists and neck. He turned towards the boat and raised his hand to signal the skipper. His buddy jumped in nearby with a splash, and the two of them swam around to the boat’s anchor line and prepared to descend.

They exchanged thumbs-down signals and pressed the release valves on their suits, venting as much air as possible. Pete clearly remembered his early days of diving when he was learning to manage his dry suit, and the embarrassment of hanging upside down in the water, helpless, as the legs and boots of the suit filled with air and his buddies laughed.

No mishaps this time: with over five hundred dives in his logbook, Pete rarely made mistakes. Suits and jackets vented, following the line of the anchor rope, the two divers inverted and finned downwards, feeling the pressure mount as they descended towards the sea floor. Pete’s ears popped as they reached double the surface pressure, then three times, then four. At thirty metres deep, the sea floor was a mixture of rock and silt, with clumps of kelp waving to and fro. Colours had faded, but the light of Pete's torch brought vivid reds and pinks to life, urchins and sunstars. A large silver fish swam idly by, ignoring the pair.

Floating gently above the sea bed, Pete looked his buddy in the eye and shrugged. Signing to each other, they set out to search the surrounding area, finning side by side as they surveyed the silt in a careful pattern radiating from the anchor.

There was nothing. Where they had expected to find a well-known shipwreck, some of the hull and boilers intact, there were only rocks. Disappointed, the two divers amused themselves for a short while chasing lobsters and crabs down a small gully, and collected an empty urchin shell, before slowly ascending by the anchor line again. They rose steadily, the pressure on their limbs reducing gradually, eyes on their dive computers, managing the gas absorption and expansion in their bodies.

From the boat, the skipper looked down and frowned as he saw clusters of bubbles breaking the surface close to the boat.

"They're on their way back up. Didn't expect them so early." He turned to the other member of the crew. "Stand by with oxygen in case there's something wrong."

Pete's hand was the first to break the surface, giving the boat the OK signal. The skipper breathed a sigh of relief, and the crewman dropped a ladder over the side. Pete handed his weights and fins up to the boat and climbed over the side. Pulling his mask off, he glared at the skipper.

"Nothing there. Not a single speck of rust. Wreck of a wooden ship carrying kelp, maybe?"

The skipper was taken aback. "No, we're right over it. The GPS co-ordinates are spot on. Look for yourself."

Pete shrugged out of his buoyancy jacket and switched off the air supply from his cylinders, stowing them securely on a rack in the middle of the boat. Joining the skipper in the tiny cabin, not much more than a box designed to shield the driver and instruments from the elements and support the boat's solar panels, they re-checked their positioning. Sure enough, the co-ordinates appeared correct.

"I don't understand. I haven't had any bother with this site before. Mind you, it's not like we have any marks to follow, out here. GPS could be on the blink, I suppose. Look, we'll waive the dive fee for today, is that alright? Let's get back to shore."

The passengers settled on benches as the boat hauled anchor and set off, cutting silently through the waves, propellers powered on this trip by the bright sun overhead. Pete was sweating in his dry suit now, the contrast between air and sea temperatures taking its toll. Gazing vacantly at the blue horizon as he swigged from a water bottle, he was perfectly placed to see the ship.

It sailed steadily towards them, a huge cargo vessel stacked with containers. Pete turned to the skipper, suddenly concerned. "We're nowhere near the main shipping lanes, are we?"

The skipper had his eyes forwards, searching for distant marks to the port. He was struggling to reconcile the GPS navigation with his knowledge of the coast. Something wasn't right.

"No, a couple of miles off." He turned briefly, and his eyes widened in horror as he saw the container ship bearing down towards them, heading for the shoreline.

"What the hell?" He grabbed the radio, still the most reliable method of communication at sea. "Red container vessel eastbound at 51.22 / 01.50, this is Manta IV on Channel 13, over."

"Manta IV, this is MV Barnard, switch to Channel 68."

"Manta switching Channel 68."

"Barnard, be advised, you have strayed from the shipping lane, over."

"Manta, our GPS shows no course deviation, over."

Pete was listening intently. "Skip, tell them the GPS may be faulty. Quickly."

"Barnard, GPS may be inaccurate, check your marks, you're heading towards the sand bars, repeat, sand bars. Over." He turned to Pete. "Is that possible? The satellites can't have moved."

Before Pete could reply, the radio squawked again. "Manta, thank you, adjusting course, over and out." They heard the distant rumble of the huge ship's emergency fossil fuel engines starting up, adding a rush of energy as it struggled to turn away from danger. The radio sounded again as the airwaves were flooded with emergency calls, and overhead they heard the clattering rotors of a coastguard drone, heading out to sea.

•

Susie was the last one into the office on Monday morning. Pete was in the middle of recounting his dramatic tale from the weekend.

"…this great big red hull bearing down on us, its engines screaming – never heard those emergency motors kick in before. We're heading backwards at fast as we can, trying to avoid the wash, boat rocking all over the place. We're off course for the port too, GPS is haywire, trying to follow the old marks into the harbour…" He paused as Susie flew through the door.

"Sorry I'm late. There was a lost drone in my street, buzzing everywhere. Navigation systems must have gone down."

"Same problem, I guess." Pete continued. "So anyway, we hear the coastguard overhead, and thought they'd sent a mayday signal, but no, it's another ship, beached on the sand bars further up the coast. All sorts of panic on the radio. Big red manages to turn and heads back to the shipping lanes, we got back to harbour and went for a stiff drink."

"Normal quiet Sunday, then, Pete," teased Joel. "A few new shipwrecks for you to dive?"

"Nah, most of them are beached on the sandbars, so they'll be re-floated. The only sinking was in the middle of the channel, too deep for me to play with. All hands safe, thank goodness."

Ross turned to Susie. "You had a lost drone this morning, huh? Pete's right, it sounds like the same problem. But why only one? If the GPS scramble has affected shipping at such a scale, why isn't every drone in London chasing its tail?"

"Probably older versions of software in some equipment. I didn't see which delivery company that drone came from. Should be able to find out. There'll be a vulnerability in there, which has hit shipping as well. Any reports from airlines?"

Noor shook her head. "Nothing on the major carriers. Military are keeping quiet, but I haven't picked up any reports of crashes or planes off course."

"That points even more clearly to a hole in some older software, then. Flight instrumentation is top priority for updates. Can't have planes falling from the sky."

"Odd target for a cyber attack, though," said Ella. "This is just mischief. There's no financial gain to be had."

Cameron shook her head. "No, this is just another disruption in the chain. More chaos building. I think we can be sure that the hurricanes have started." She thought for a moment. "Let's work out a shorthand for each attack so we're clear where we are. Joel, they use common names for the tropical storms, don't they? What shall we use?"

"Coffee brands," joked Sandeep.

"Rugby players," suggested Joel.

"Film stars," said Ella.

"Bands," said Susie.

"Has to be something international," said Cameron. "I'll be running this through the forums."

"Can't use brand names or countries," replied Joel. "That would be too confusing. How about authors. Politicians. Scientists?"

"Scientists. I like scientists. What've we got?" Cameron pulled up a wiki on screen.

"A – Ayrton? Hertha Ayrton. Electric arcs and sand ripples. Nice. Okay, the first 'storm' was this business with the chatbots, all that propaganda stirring up the crowds." Cameron opened her forum account, cloaking the location out of habit. "I'll publish these live. Next?"

"B – Becquerel?" suggested Noor. "Henri Becquerel. Nobel prize for evidence of radioactivity. What was the second attack?"

"I guess it would be the Distributed Denial of Service attack on the credentialing blockchain," replied Pete. "That was a bit of a mess. What was it again, a botnet of smart fridges? I'll never trust mine again. Lucky the team over in Beijing sorted it out quickly."

"Okay, DDoS attack is Storm Becquerel." Cameron added a line to her forum post. "What was the third one? Do we count the hack on the airline flight management systems?"

"Oh, I think so," replied Ross. "It was simple and short lived, but it was high profile. I'm surprised you got back from the Emirates with your luggage. People were stranded for days, and there are still bags circling the world, from what I hear. That's our C. Who's it going to be?"

"Marie Curie. Got to be," said Susie.

"Two Nobel prizes, can't fault that," replied Ross with a rare grin. "Storm Curie for the flights."

"So this GPS problem is our fourth attack, then? Our D."

"Has anyone worked out the vulnerability yet?" asked Pete.

"Plenty of people working on it. Susie, we need to get a lead on that drone's delivery company, we should be able to get the details of the attack from their systems. Pete, could you find out the software used on your dive boat. By all accounts there was a huge panic at NASA and Roscosmos," continued Cameron, "but as there wasn't a universal effect, they're pretty sure there are no compromises with the satellites. Looks like some sort of glitch in the receivers."

"Okay, definitely our D. Darwin?" suggested Ella. She grinned sidelong at Pete. "Although with you reversing the evolutionary path, Pete, land back to water, it's a strange choice."

Pete threw a table tennis ball at her. She caught it and threw it back with a deft flick of the wrist. Pete mishandled the catch, and the ball ricocheted off the wall behind and bounced in the middle of the table. Joel snatched it out of the air, laughing.

Cameron glanced at the time. "Okay folks, we have clients to see. Ross, you and I can have a look at those

GPS vulnerabilities when we get our hands on the software. See if we can get the fix out first, maintain our good reputation."

They scattered, eager to get on with their work.

•

The team worked late through the summer evening, analysing the delivery drone's navigation system and the download from Pete's dive boat charter. As the day wore on, reports of more serious accidents had emerged over the news channels and through online communities, the effects rippling out worldwide.

In the end, the breakthrough came. The Argentum team were first to the finishing line, another feather in their caps. The grateful courier service retrieved its lost drones. The software company behind the flawed systems rapidly updated its clients' systems. Cameron uploaded the patch for the other teams battling the same challenge.

"Even the most up to date software has holes in it, if you look carefully," sighed Sandeep. "It's wide open."

"We'll recommend urgent updates. Get some details out there, Sandeep. Push the whole industry to get their house in order."

Ross finally left the office at dusk, collecting his bike, and waving briefly to Cameron and Sandeep as he rode towards the river and home. He cycled far enough to be sure he was out of sight, and turned off his normal route, dismounting at the gate to a secluded green space.

Propping his bike against a tree, he wandered along a path, his feet crunching on the gravel. The little park was deserted. Perfect.

Pulling out a burner smartscreen – a cheap device that could be disposed of, thrown away at the first sign of detection – he initiated a call. Moments later, it was answered: still no face on the screen. The other party remained anonymous. The synthesised voice grated on his nerves.

"We have noticed new speculation around the manipulation of cryptocurrencies."

Ross winced. "Uh, I haven't seen that. Look, there are plenty of good people working on these threats. Someone else will have come up with the same theory independently."

There was no response.

He blustered on. "That's how it works, you know that. Lots of teams, lots of experts all over the world. Sometimes we get the first fix, sometimes other people. We all work together."

"Accepted. You have something to report?"

"Uh, yes. We're looking at the recent navigation system failures. We've identified a vulnerability in older software that was compromised to scramble GPS signals. It was an easy breach. The fix is out there and confirmed by other teams. We're recommending updates across the board for all navigation systems going forward, as there seem to be a number of other bits of dodgy code where attacks could be initiated."

“Good.”

Ross was puzzled. “I don’t understand where you’re coming from. Every time we find a fix for an attack, we make sure updates are rolled out to close down the route to future hacks. Every time I report in, you’re pleased, you tell me to recommend more updates. How does this benefit you?”

“You do not need to know. You have done well. Continue.”

The connection terminated. Ross was left standing alone in the encroaching darkness of the park.

10: TURNING UP THE HEAT

Charlie could hear the commotion from the top of the stairs. Hurrying down to the kitchen, he found the children in uproar.

"I told the screen to put cartoons on and it said it doesn't like them. It won't switch over from the news," wailed Tara.

"My school forum's all messed up. My friends have disappeared and I can see all the teachers' messages. There's swearing!" declared an appalled Nina.

Dilan said nothing; he was getting on with his breakfast.

Charlie tried ineffectively to calm his daughters down. "Don't worry, it'll just be a little glitch in the system. These things happen."

The wailing redoubled.

"You've all got holiday club today, aren't you excited? Visit to the canal museum? A ride through the tunnel?"

Nina rolled her eyes. "Oh dad, really? I've been before. It's going to be so dull."

Sameena came bustling in. "Come on, you three, aren't you ready yet? The bus will be here soon. Dilan, no, you can't have thirds, go and clean your teeth. Nina, have you drunk your milk? Tara, why are you wearing that dress? I said shorts and a t-shirt. Go and get changed, quickly."

She threw her hands up in mock horror. "Children. It's like herding cats."

They all jumped as the screen changed and started blasting out rock music, strobe lights flashing.

"Who did that?" cried Charlie. "Off! Off!"

The screen was unresponsive. Sameena marched over and fiddled around the back of the device, searching for a manual override. Finally, she found it, and the room fell mercifully silent.

"Well, that was a wake-up call. Must get Cameron to have a look at it when she comes up this weekend."

"Oh, don't bother her, Charlie. She's supposed to be relaxing. I'm looking forward to meeting Ben. I'm so glad she's bringing him to meet us at last."

Charlie grinned. "It'll be good if she's found someone who can keep up with her. She won't mind looking at the screen, though. Especially if it keeps the kids quiet."

A hoot from the road outside heralded the otherwise silent arrival of the bus. Sameena rushed out of the kitchen, chivvying the children up and shepherding them out of the front door. "Have a lovely day." She watched and waved as they took their seats and the bus pulled off up the hill, then she turned back to the house.

"Peace at last."

Charlie swigged the last of his coffee. "Right, I'll be off. Quarterly board meeting today. Should be pretty smooth, we've had a few good months." He kissed Sameena and picked up his bag. His wife reached for the dog's leash, and an excited Roxy joined them as they left the house together.

•

Ross tossed and turned. He was having trouble sleeping. Was it the pressure of work, the pressure of training, or the terrible feelings of failure and betrayal that gnawed at his guts? He had lost weight since the high of his last, triumphant, race. The summer sun never touched his pale complexion, making his gaunt visage stand out even more. He did not know how this might end.

Tangled in the twisted sheet, sweating profusely, he struggled to free himself and went to open a window, desperate for air. This was the hottest night he could remember. The sun was already up, but it was still very early. There was no sound of footsteps on the street, no whirr of drone rotors to be heard. Flinging open the window, he gasped as cool air hit him. How strange. Turning back towards his bed, he brushed against a radiator. It was burning hot.

"Heating off." There was no acknowledgement from the house portal. "Heating off." Swearing, Ross pulled on a pair of underpants and opened his bedroom door. Where the hell were the kill switches? He tried the portal again. "Heating off."

Feeling his way down the wall of the hall, he racked his brains. When his mum redecorated, they'd taken out all the ugly, obsolete light switches and plastered over the holes.

For years now, sensors in lightbulbs simply switched them on when you entered a room, and off when you left. With the heating on voice control, and reacting intelligently to the environment, there was no need for a manual switch. Somewhere, though, there had been the original controls, the override for the heating system. They had been too complex to remove, still connected to the circuits that were not controlled by the portal, so instead they'd carved a hole for it in the wall, pushed it deep inside, and papered over the gap.

His hands glided over the paper, much shabbier than it had been ten years ago. Fingertips explored dips in the plaster beneath. It had been around here somewhere…

Success. Ross felt a regular rectangular dip in the wall. After another desperate shout at the portal which elicited no response, he took a deep breath of the stifling air and tore into the paper, trying to make a neat flap with his fingers, hoping to cause as little mess as possible. The control panel appeared. Flipping its cover off, he saw lights beneath. There was the slider, the kill switch that he sought. Stiff with years of neglect, it took Ross some effort to push it to the off position, but finally it clicked into place. Ross sighed and closed the control panel cover, then ineffectively tried to fold back the torn flap of wallpaper. Hopefully that would kill the heating.

He shook his head ruefully. Well, he was up now. Time for a cold shower. He'd be in the office early.

•

"Have we all been following the reports of portal and screen failures?" asked Cameron as the team met for their morning catch-up.

There was a chorus of assent.

"There's been some disruption to a few private communities, too. Some software they use in the education sector," added Ella. "We've had a call from the developers to give them a hand finding the fix."

"That's good," grinned Cameron. Charlie had been on the phone before his meeting. "My niece got caught up in that. I'm not sure she was ready to find out how her teachers think."

"The bloody heating was the one that got me," complained Ross. "Barely slept. Ridiculous trick in the middle of summer. And now the aircon's off in here. Where's this come from?"

"Same place as the rest, what do you think?" Joel was getting more and more irritated by Ross's attitude.

"Is this our E then? Storm Edison, anyone?" Noor tried to keep the peace.

"Whatever." They were all fractious with the heat. There was something simmering in the air.

"Let's crack on with our contracts." Cameron realised splitting them up would reduce the friction. "Get some fresh air, get out to see clients, make the most of the nice weather."

They didn't take much persuading. Only Ella and Susie opted to stay in the stifling office, working on their financial models. Ross made his way east to see the delivery company and check up on their drone navigation updates. Joel and Noor made their way north to the community software developers, to help unscramble their user accounts. Pete had an appointment at Lloyds of London to discuss insurance claims arising from the GPS receiver failures.

Sandeep followed up a call to the airport, working with an airline that was still tidying up from the flight information hack. Although the team had identified the system weakness, a new breach had exploited the vulnerability they'd discovered before they had a chance to deploy their fix. It had been frustrating for Sandeep and for the client, and continued to disrupt passengers across the world.

Cameron made it her business to call on the national portal provider. She needed some insights into the latest attack. Leaving the office, she walked the short distance to the river, where a ferry was just pulling in. That would be a cool way to travel, out in the middle of the Thames. She boarded the broad, flat vessel and joined a group of tourists at the stern for the short journey upriver to Westminster pier.

As they approached the bridge, Cameron could hear shouting. A large demonstration was taking place outside Parliament. She climbed up from the pier towards Big Ben. The square in front of the Palace of Westminster was crowded with people waving placards as statues of Churchill, Mandela, Lincoln, Gandhi and other great statesmen gazed impassively upon them. The protestors were agitated, the police presence heavy. As Cameron watched, the demonstrators broke the police cordon, rushing towards the palace. Shouting, sirens, and the sound of taser drones filled the air. Cameron started to run towards Whitehall and Trafalgar Square, the crowd surging towards her. She changed direction and turned down a side street, back towards the river, adrenaline pumping.

The cumulative effect of social media propaganda and polarisation of society, the annoyance of failures of flights and deliveries, the inconvenience of failing portals, and the extreme heat, had pushed the city to the limit. The fallout had just begun.

•

"...Business news now, and the pound has fallen sharply against the Bitcoin today after further concerns over the government's reactions to recent far-right demonstrations. The pound remains stable against the Dollar, Euro, Yen and Yuan which have also seen falls due to political unrest. All cryptocurrencies remain strong..."

Sir Simon Winchester, the bank's chief executive, turned away from the screens on the wall of the boardroom and glowered at his team of analysts.

"So, after posting the best quarter on record, a few hard-right idiots are mucking about with the markets. There's talk of downgrading the country's credit rating. What's kicked all this off?"

The analysts glanced at each other nervously. One of them spoke up.

"This movement wasn't predicted by any of our models. We haven't seen a swing like this for two decades. You have to go back to pre-crypto days to find any fiscal upheaval on this scale. It takes a major external influence to have this kind of effect. Even the terrorist activity in the early part of the millennium didn't cause this much disruption."

Sir Simon sighed. "These things are always transitory. No one can destabilise a whole currency system, and god knows they've tried for decades. I don't think anyone's gotten close since Soros shorted the market in '92. Made him millions, though." For a moment, he was lost in thought. "Okay, thanks for the heads up, keep monitoring the situation. Any unusual trades on hard or cryptocurrency, I need to know straight away. Pay particular attention to futures."

The analysts trooped out, and Sir Simon turned to the screen. "Reception. Get Bill up here."

A few minutes later, Bill appeared at the door. The chief executive was alone, lounging in a tan leather chair, watching the monitors as waves of green and red swept across the central screens, showing the rise and fall of stocks and shares. To the side, another feed showed currency movements, the value of the pound against hard and cryptocurrencies, in real time.

The central screens were, in the main, green. Some of the graphs to the right were dropping.

Bill took in the scene and frowned. "What's up?"

The Sir Simon swung upright and gestured for him to sit. "Your cyber security team. Ms Silvera and her crew. Good operatives."

Bill nodded in agreement, wondering where this was going.

"They've been in and out updating the systems, haven't they? And they did a good job on the ransomware attack back in the Spring."

"Yes, as you know there's been a tipoff about a wave of attacks. Looking at the chaos out there, I think they may have started. Cameron and her team have patched and strengthened all of our older systems, we've completed a full round of training, and our software upgrades are bang up to date."

Sir Simon smiled, approvingly. "Good. They are a talented group, and farsighted. I was particularly interested in their findings around currency manipulation and profits from Bitcoin futures. Who identified this element of the last attack?"

"Ah, yes, that would be Ella Stanford." Bill smiled. "She's good. Used to work in the City, professionally qualified, knows her stuff."

"I think she's onto something. These market movements are unusual. The value of cryptocurrencies is rising, more quickly and more smoothly than the economic conditions would suggest. I can't unilaterally suspend trading, but I can be ready, and make sure my peers are also prepared. Can you contact the Argentum team? I want to speak to her."

"Yes, sir. I'll place a call now."

"Good. And have your staff on alert for anything unusual in the markets or on our systems. There's a storm coming. I can feel it in my bones."

•

Cameron was back in the office when Ben called. "Hey, babe. You busy?"

"Ah, crikey, I nearly got caught in that fuss over at Parliament Square. Very scary."

"Are you okay?" Ben sounded concerned.

"Yeah, calmed down now, thanks. Looking forward to getting out of London for the weekend. What are you after? You getting second thoughts about coming up to the village? Charlie's not that scary."

Ben laughed. "From what I've heard, it's Aunt Vicky and her cat I should be more frightened of. No, this is work related. Something you might know more about than me. There's something odd going on with our systems. We have a big network of intelligent sensors feeding back data to our design centre, and they're all going offline. There's no problems reported on the network. All connections good."

Cameron sat up straight, concerned. "That's odd. You're right. Tell me a bit more about these sensors."

"Most of the stuff we design has sensors built into the print. For instance, a component may have a way of tracking wear and tear and the data comes back to us. If there's a problem, we can improve the design, or the spec of the materials."

Cameron knew the type of feedback loop he described. Simple, unobtrusive use of what was once called 'the Internet of Things' to optimise manufacturing processes and service customers more effectively. Commendable stuff.

She thought carefully. "So, let me get this right, the sensors look as if they are offline at your end. They're not sending data back, although the network is sound."

"That's right."

"Can you test any sensors? See what they're processing?"

"We don't touch them. The manufacturing companies take our designs and the sensors are printed along with the components. Pretty neat, huh? But no, I can't get hold of any easily."

"They're part of the 3D printing process, you say? That's interesting. I'll have a chat with Charlie. See whether any of the components they produce have a similar feature."

"Good idea. This is pretty standard in the industry. There'll be some sort of equivalent in his designs. What are you thinking? I bet you've come up with the answer already."

"Hmm. Maybe. Those little sensors may not be much, but put them together and you have a lot of processing power. Could be nothing, but after the last few weeks I don't know what's coming next. The Speakeasy crew have some imagination, I'll give them that."

"Okay babe, thanks, I have to go. I'll see you tonight."

Ben terminated the call, and Cameron sat, thoughtful, her eyes unfocused. Her flash of intuition was disturbing. What storm had been unleashed this time?

•

Ella and Susie arrived at the bank in response to Bill's call. They were ushered straight up to the boardroom where he was waiting. "Sir Simon Winchester – Ella Stanford, Susie Lu."

"Good afternoon, Ms Stanford, Ms Lu. Thank you for coming so promptly." The chief executive paused. "I believe that in your investigations into the Speakeasy cyber attack in April, you identified a pattern of market behaviour that enable the perpetrators to profit."

Ella nodded. "Yes, sir, I've modelled that period completely and I've been watching the markets since then. Cryptocurrency is rising again. Of course, it has a history of fluctuations. It's not necessarily the precursor to an attack."

Sir Simon shook his head. "This feels different. Yes, cryptocurrency is rising against the pound and dollar, and fluctuations are not unknown. But every hard currency is falling. This is unprecedented."

Susie stepped forwards. "We have serious concerns." She glanced at Ella, and continued. "We have identified a series of different styles of attack which have cumulatively weakened the global economy and standing of incumbent political parties. The cyber security community has named them in the style of tropical storms."

Sir Simon nodded. "Very good. Please continue."

"The first one we noted was Storm Ayrton: social media manipulation. There was a sharp increase in 'bot traffic across social networks worldwide in May, and the high level of interference has been sustained. People think they're talking to other humans when they're actually talking to machines. The machines have been trained to provoke disruption and polarisation of opinion. That's the origin of this build-up of demonstrations and political fuss over the last three months."

"That makes a lot of sense," Bill interjected. "This unrest puts pressure on the government to resolve it, uses up resources." He looked closer at the flickering green and red numbers on the stocks screen. "Interesting, some of the highest valued London stocks at the moment are in defence and infrastructure. That fits."

"What else have you observed, Ms Lu?" asked Sir Simon.

"Okay, around the time that Storm Ayrton began, there was a low-level Distributed Denial of Service attack on some credentialing servers. Cameron picked up on this when she flew back from the Emirates. We called this Storm Becquerel. A simultaneous exploitation of vulnerable flight management software caused delays and upheaval worldwide: that's Storm Curie. Then there were the shipwrecks and drones going astray after the GPS hack: Darwin. We're up to Storm Edison so far with the reported portal failures. They still haven't been resolved."

"Thank you, yes, I see." Sir Simon paused. "A steady wave of attacks. Very interesting. Do you anticipate these continuing? Do you have any insight into the source?"

Ella looked resigned and worried. "We have some idea of where this is coming from, but other than fighting each wave and making sure that defences are solid, there is very little we can do. As Susie says, if this currency movement is genuinely down to manipulation of society through social networks and environmental irritations, then it's highly possible we are seeing the start of something bigger."

Stepping forward, Bill sought to reassure them all. "Systems are as tight as a drum down there. All the upgrades are complete. If we start seeing unusual trades, is there any way we can stop them?"

Sir Simon shook his head. "All we can hope is that the movements are steady. If there's a run on futures, and the prices hold, there's no profit to be taken. Ms Stanford, what is your view on possible manipulation in the opposite direction."

Ella composed herself. She'd run the scenarios with Cameron.

"Hard currency is falling because of a loss of confidence in the sovereign states," she said. "There are threats to reduce national credit ratings, for instance. It's taken weeks to get to this stage, drip-feeding polarising propaganda and provoking unrest."

"Yes," agreed Sir Simon. "Only a sustained campaign of

this type could have such a significant effect. However, is it not true that a reversal of sentiment will also take time?"

Ella nodded in agreement. "If this manipulation is the work of our Speakeasy perpetrators, they can't artificially reverse sentiment quickly enough to have an acute effect on valuations. However, if they have a way of suddenly reducing confidence in cryptocurrency, that's a different matter. It worked in April because there was a single attack that induced loss of confidence in the whole system for a very short period of time. I can't see a way for them to do this globally unless they have another worm ready to roll, and our industry has worked hard to tighten up all the critical systems. Unless…" she tailed off.

"Unless what?" prompted Bill.

"Unless… there is a compromise already built in."

Susie put her hand to her mouth. She was pale. "Oh god. Is that why they gave us the warning? They knew we would strengthen defences. We had to."

The chief executive looked from one to the other. "What are you saying? Surely if you've built defences then the attackers have to rely on human error to exploit new vulnerabilities."

Ella shook her head. "Quite the opposite. They are relying on professionals like us to do their jobs. What if the updates we've applied were already compromised? What if the work we've done – all of us, worldwide – has thrown the systems wide open?"

•

The summer weather had set in for August. While London was suffering from the heat, with pockets of protest and unrest disrupting the capital and stretching the police to the limit, the countryside basked calmly in glorious warmth.

The vines growing around the village had ripened, and tall tractors with impossibly thin wheels rolled through the fields, shaking grapes from the plants and delivering them to the sorting shed. There, high-speed cameras again took the place of centuries of human expertise, detecting the precise ripeness and sugar content of each fruit, choosing only the best for the ancient champagne houses. This year's crop had the look of a vintage, a rare millésime; even the local fizz produced from the poorer quality grapes was expected to be excellent.

Cameron and Ben strolled hand in hand down the footpath that skirted the vines, as Roxy strained on her leash. She knew there was a run coming and dragged her dawdling humans along the familiar route as fast as possible. Reaching the stile to an empty field, Cameron let the dog off her leash. Roxy wriggled through under the fence, as Ben and Cameron climbed up the protruding cross-pieces of the stile and over to the other side. They watched as Roxy scampered here and there, chasing her tail, poking her nose down rabbit holes, and leaving her mark on the fences and hedgerows. Cameron could see white wind turbines in the distance, barely moving, bright against the cloudless blue sky. Today the country's electricity came from the power of the sun.

Barbecue smoke wafted on a light breeze from a nearby garden. Ben sniffed appreciatively. "Smells good."

Cameron gave him a playful punch on the arm. "You've just had breakfast, you can't be hungry again. We'll get our barbecue this evening." She looked around the fields and sighed. "I love this place. I miss the steady pace of life."

"Bit quiet for me," admitted Ben. "I can see how you ended up spending all your time with computers. I was always out doing things with my hands, born engineer. It's nice to be here, though," he added quickly, dodging another poke, as Cameron laughed.

A large drone flew overhead, laden with goods. Startled, Roxy barked at it until it disappeared between houses and into the village.

"It's nice to see you relax," Ben continued. "You've had a hellish few weeks. All sorted now?"

"It never ends." Cameron looked ruefully at him. "We're running to keep up with security updates for clients, there are phishing emails flying everywhere, and these random attacks are just getting more and more intense. No sooner have we defused one than another pops up. It's the same all over the world."

"Surely the defensive work you're doing is having some impact?" Ben was concerned. Cameron was under a lot of stress.

"Hard to tell. We're finding weaknesses and patching them, but we've had repeat attacks that come along straight away and exploit the weakness we found before the patch goes in. It's almost as if there's someone watching and reacting to what we do, pushing us to get security updates in as fast as possible."

She was thoughtful for a moment. The idea that someone in the cyber security community was involved in the attacks had occurred to her before. She pushed it to the back of her mind again. Something to address later.

She was brought back to earth suddenly by a crash of metal from the direction of the village. Startled, she looked up, and heard shouting.

"The drone's gone down. Roxy! Roxy!" she whistled frantically. "Here, Roxy!"

They ran down a path towards the village, Roxy at their heels, and arrived at a scene of devastation. The delivery drone had veered off course, crashing into a passing autocar. Villagers were working together to try and free the trapped passenger, the car's wheels spinning as it tried to continue on its way. Boxes, glass and debris were scattered on the road, and the drone was embedded in the side of the car, its rotors warped and bent. Ben stepped in and helped to disable the autocar's power system. The wheels stopped whirring, locks holding the far door clicked open, and the shocked passenger climbed out, shaking, and bleeding from myriad tiny glass shards.

Cameron triggered the recovery alert on the drone, looking anxiously into the sky.

Ben joined her. "I know what you're thinking. Is this a one-off? Or are there more."

She nodded. "It's very unusual for a drone to fail. There

were a few navigation problems with the GPS attack that caused all those ships to run aground."

"Storm Darwin?" interjected Ben.

"Yes, that's the one. The affected drones just flew around in circles, completely lost. Ross and I found the fix for that particular vulnerability. I wonder what this is. Interference with the local signal, maybe?" She pulled out her smartscreen and scanned the net for news.

"Nothing else reported, yet, but it's only been a few minutes. Let's go and see Andy. He may have more information."

The two of them headed up the hill towards Andy's house. Aunt Vicky met them half way up.

"Cameron, darling, what was that noise? Oh… this must be Ben, how lovely to meet you." Distracted from the crash, Aunt Vicky's attention was focused on the young man. "I'm looking forward to a nicc long chat with you at the barbecue this afternoon."

Ben shook her hand warmly and smiled. Aunt Vicky looked pleased.

Cameron took Ben's arm. "We were just popping up to see Andy. Is he in, Aunt Vicky?"

"I think so, darling, I saw him come back from walking Jasper about half an hour ago."

"Great, thanks. We'll see you at the barbecue." Cameron ushered Ben up the hill, and knocked on Andy's door.

Andy's welcome was effusive. "Cameron. Good to see you. What was that racket earlier? And who is this young man?"

"Ben – Andy. Drone crashed down on the high street. Took out an autocar. Any other reports like that?"

Andy looked startled. "That's unusual." He snapped his fingers at the screen on the wall and it sprang to life, displaying the raw news feeds that formed the building blocks of reporting. Selecting map view and narrowing down the report time to the current day, clusters of incidents appeared on the screen.

"There you go. Reports from today. Let's have a look." He drilled down into a cluster pinpointed on the Midlands. "There's the crash in the village. Look, four more reported within a ten-kilometre radius." He zoomed back out.

Cameron and Ben watched, fascinated, as more pinpoints popped onto the screen, each one a reported incident. Andy drilled into a few clusters at random. "All drones."

Cameron put her head in her hands. "I don't believe it. We've just rolled out drone software updates. How the hell have they been attacked so quickly? We just can't keep up."

"Another storm?" asked Andy quietly.

Cameron nodded. "I guess that's our F. We agreed on Franklin. I'd better get online." She looked at Ben soberly. "That wasn't what I'd planned for this weekend."

He hugged her. "Don't worry. I understand. It can't be helped. You get to work. I'll keep Aunt Vicky at bay and play with the kids for you. At least you can do this from here. You don't need to go back to London."

Andy looked concerned. "Is there anything I can do to help?"

“Get something out on the news, Andy. Warn people to keep watch for drones out of control. Ask for the public to be vigilant for anything else unusual. This is building up to something huge.”

11: INTO THE BLUE

The worm had been roused from its slumber. Parameters deep in its code found their mark, matching, against a pre-ordained date string, the heartbeat of the servers in which it slept. It had travelled the world, spreading its progeny into every corner of the web, into every network it could penetrate.

Its creators watched in the shadows. They had nudged their master plan forward in real life while the worm spread in the virtual world. Their bots were trolling public sentiment in every country, in every language, across every community forum. Lightning attacks from their Dark Web contractors had increased unrest and destabilised political powers. Operatives on the ground enabled them to gain control of people who could help to ensure the malicious code reached its mark. Compromised threat intelligence operatives were doing their bidding, appearing to strengthen cyber defences while inadvertently assisting the spread of the worm.

It was time.

•

Bill was surprised when the call alert sounded; he was enjoying his weekend off. He was even more shocked to see his chief executive's face on the screen.

"Sir Simon, how can I help you?"

"Bill, the activity we anticipated has begun. Could you alert Ms Stanford and Ms Silvera. No more discussion over open networks."

The call went dead.

Futures trading. Bill hauled himself out of the deckchair in which he had been lounging, and went into his house. He flicked on the wall screen and pulled up the live cryptocurrency market details. Sure enough, the volume of futures trades had risen above its normal level. Broadening the date range, the graphs they had been following suddenly made sense. The gradual climb in volume, with hindsight, had started weeks before, but had been carefully disguised.

Bill called Ella Stanford first. "Good afternoon, Ella, apologies for the weekend call. The activity we discussed has reached the warning threshold."

On the other end of the call, Ella's eyes widened, and she nodded.

"Understood. I'll be there in an hour. I'll bring Susie as well."

Bill, Ella and Susie arrived at the bank within a few minutes of each other. Sir Simon's plush autocar stood at the door. The streets were deserted. A combination of concern over drone accidents, damage from the last few days' unrest, and businesses being closed as normal for the weekend meant that there were few people out in the city.

The three of them passed through the security checks and the barrier in the foyer, and made their way up the sweeping, carpeted stairs to the now-familiar boardroom. Sir Simon was sitting in his usual leather chair, gazing ruefully at the monitors on the wall. An untouched cup of coffee sat in front of him of the table. He turned towards the door as Bill, Ella and Susie entered.

"Bill, Ms Stanford, Ms Lu, thank you for coming so promptly. Do you have any word from Ms Silvera?"

Ella stepped forwards. "I've spoken to her. She's not in London this weekend; she's out in the country visiting family. She's busy looking into what we've dubbed Storm Franklin, the latest drone malfunctions that are causing major incidents."

Sir Simon nodded. "That's fine, she doesn't need to be here. I've alerted my counterparts in the industry. We are endeavouring to suspend cryptocurrency futures, but the timing could not be neater. Although we are all aware that crypto markets never close, the mere fact that this has reached a peak at a weekend has caught many institutions off guard."

"Not you, though," said Bill.

Sir Simon smiled.

"If it were I who planned this strategy, and I had the ability to time its execution precisely, I would ensure that it happened at the most inconvenient point for those who may try to stop me."

Susie gave him an irreverent grin. "Very good. You may have a future in cyber security, Sir Simon."

The bank's chief executive laughed. "This has certainly been an eye-opener." He adopted a more serious tone. "This is just the start, though. It's the next step that worries me. How are they going to force the price back down and take their profits? That's the real challenge."

He sighed. "Suspending trading may reduce their profits, but it's a drop in the ocean. Where the hell will it go from here?"

•

Ross stared at the news channel, horrified. The information he had passed on about dronc weaknesses had seemed innocent at the time. The speed at which the second attack had hit all the drone systems was astounding. He was absolutely certain that the failures being reported could only have come from a fast exploit of the vulnerability he'd exposed.

How the hell had they managed to deploy the attack, though? How could the malicious code have dropped so fast? It was one thing writing a quick exploit to take down the drones, but quite another to make sure it appeared in their operating systems. They would have to have access to the servers that controlled the drones. Either they already did – in which case, why did the GPS scramble not hit everyone? – or something had changed recently.

Ross went cold. The updates. They'd recommended security updates. The strangers in the shadows had pushed for them to happen. What if the updates themselves were compromised?

He scrambled for his smartscreen and placed a call to Cameron. She answered quickly. Behind her on the screen, he could see faded, brightly patterned wallpaper, and bright sunshine coming through a dormer window.

"Ross? What's up? Aren't you training?"

"Training's finished. Cameron, these drone crashes…"

"Storm Franklin, Ross. They're all over the place."

"I know, I've seen the news."

"Yeah, Andy's done a good job getting that out there."

"Look, Cameron, you know that vulnerability we picked up when we were analysing the GPS scramble? Is this attack exploiting that exact code error?"

"Yes, I think so. I'm working on it now. I've managed to get hold of a copy of the operating system. The thing I don't get, is that we advised security updates and they seem to have been applied. The one I'm looking at had the latest version."

Ross took a deep breath. "What if the updates were compromised? Cameron, what if the malicious code was delivered direct from the update servers?"

Cameron stared at him, horrified. "Ella and Susie had the same thought about updates at the bank. We had no evidence. Ross, we need to get upstream to the main drone operating system providers. Can you follow that up?" She paused. "What I don't understand is how they could have found and reacted to that vulnerability so quickly? No one on the forums had picked it up before us. We haven't published the details. What are we up against?"

Ross swallowed hard. "Cameron… I need to talk to you…" He shook his head. "No, it's alright. I'll get on with the drone people."

The call terminated.

Cameron sat back, startled.

Breathing hard, Ross put down his smartscreen and buried his head in his hands. The lies and deceit were catching up with him.

Thinking fast, he placed a call to Joel, phrasing it carefully. "I'm coming over to your place. Get the kettle on." He grabbed a rucksack and filled it with some spare clothes, a few packs of energy gels, and a bottle of water. He left the two smartscreens, his own and the burner device, on the table. Helmet on, he collected his bike, and the house door locked behind him. Ross pedalled away steadily towards Joel's neighbourhood.

He had been gone for almost twenty minutes when the stranger's autocar pulled up outside the house.

•

Ella, Susie, Bill and Sir Simon were still deep in discussion in the bank's boardroom.

Sir Simon turned to Ella. "How could the value of

cryptocurrency be destabilised rapidly and accurately, without also closing down trading? That's the question. It's all very well making the value fall, but these people will want to complete their trades and take their profits."

Ella pulled her notes up on her screen. "During the Speakeasy attack, there was a brief loss of confidence in banking systems. That caused the small drop in cryptocurrency values that we saw after the trading peak."

"Do you think they'd try that again?" asked Bill. "A bit obvious, isn't it? They know we're watching this time."

"Hmm, not so sure," replied Ella. "There was some odd activity on the forums, apparently, when Ross published my original findings. The consensus in the end was that there was not enough evidence to back up the assumptions. I disagree."

"How interesting," said Sir Simon. "Your analysis was perfectly accurate and well supported. There would be no reason to discredit it. However, that may explain the difficulty I have had persuading my counterparts elsewhere to take the suspension of trading seriously."

Susie chipped in. "I'm still concerned about the motivation behind their warning. It gave us the opportunity to strengthen defences, but what if there was something already planted to enable an attack?"

"Yes, you thought there may have been a vulnerability in the updates that have been rolled out, didn't you," agreed Bill. "Why don't you have a look at the code that came down the line? I can set you up a quarantine machine to work on."

"Good idea," replied Ella. "I'll see if Sandeep can join us. He's got a good eye for this sort of thing." She went to place a call on her screen, but Sir Simon held up a warning hand.

"Wait. If they have planned this so carefully, I have no doubt that some communications networks are unsafe. In fact, I would trust very few things right now. Use my personal screen." He unrolled a small device from his pocket and handed it to Ella. "That may be safer. Be careful what you say."

He turned to Bill. "We're going to need provisions. This team can't work on an empty stomach. Go and do some shopping, Bill. No drone deliveries."

Bill nodded and left the room, closing the heavy oak door behind him.

Sir Simon looked at the two girls. "How many other systems have been updated? Could this be a blanket disruption of many things to impact overall confidence in anything automated? That strategy would also afford the perpetrators cover, create enough chaos to make good their escape, as it were."

Ella looked helpless. "Well, everything. We have clients in transport. Drone systems, obviously. Utilities and power. All sorts. Multiply that by every threat team across the world – it's huge."

"We can expect some major disruption, then." Sir Simon sighed. "Ms Stanford, while your colleagues start on the analysis, would you accompany me to Downing Street? The Prime Minister needs to hear this."

•

Cameron looked drawn and pale when she finally descended from her attic. The family, and Ben, were out in the garden enjoying the sunshine. As she wandered, blinking, out of the patio doors onto the terrace, Charlie looked up. "How's it going, Cam?"

She smiled wanly. "It's getting serious. I think I know why the drones have gone down. That's the easy part. The tough bit is, we don't know exactly how the code was delivered. And Ross… something odd's going on with Ross…" Cameron shook her head.

Ben beckoned her over. "Come and sit down. You need a break."

She smiled, and joined him on a little bench seat in the shade of a large tree. Charlie poured her a glass of wine and brought a plate of snacks. She felt the stress recede.

Stretching her aching back, she yawned. "I'm going to have to get back to London. I think this is going to explode. We've been waiting for the big one. It feels like we're close."

Ben gave her shoulders a squeeze. "We can get the train tonight, if you like."

Cameron nodded. Charlie and Sameena were quiet.

Over the sound of the children and their friends

playing in a remote corner of the garden, they heard a voice calling.

"Cameron? Charlie?" Around the corner of the house came Jasper, straining on his leash, closely followed by Andy. He bent down and released the dog, who rushed off to find his friend.

"Glass of wine, Andy?" Charlie grabbed another garden seat and pulled it into the shade.

"Thanks, Charlie. That'd be lovely. Cameron, something you should see." He pulled out his smartscreen. "This just came through. We have a permanent camera monitoring Number Ten Downing Street. On normal Sundays, we just get the cat going out for a walk. Today, the Prime Minister has visitors. Look. Isn't that Ella?"

Cameron gasped. "Yes. And that's Sir Simon Winchester."

Andy stared. "Of course. I recognise him now."

Charlie looked from his sister to his friend, concerned. "Who?"

"He's the chief executive of the bank. This can mean only one thing. The trading patterns we anticipated have started. The hurricane's coming." She stood up, suddenly distressed.

"Why hasn't Ella called? What's going on?" She reached for her screen.

Andy held out a warning hand. "Is it safe to call? Forum manipulation, hacks, drones, and now the bank. How far does this spread?"

Cameron grinned at him. "Yes, you're right, but I have

an idea. There's something I want to try. Andy, I may need your help."

"What for?"

"I'm going to build our own end-to-end messaging system, but it will mean disrupting some of the public networks. Can you get something out on the news channels? Tell people not to panic, that normal service will be resumed, say it's scheduled maintenance overrunning or something."

"Wow. That's heavy-handed, isn't it?"

"Not really, Andy, in the circumstances. And I'm only talking about the Bluetooth network." She smiled. "I'm going to build a mesh network. Better let the team know – they're probably expecting it." She bent over her screen. "Right. Careful wording…"

'Hi Ella, are you lunching with Simon? Get your teeth into a good blue steak.' She hit send.

"Let's see if that works." The reply came almost by return.

"Aha! Let's see. 'Yes, Susie and Sandeep here too. Chatting about the future. Speak to you shortly.'" Cameron grinned.

"Excellent, that's three of them already at the bank, and we know that Sir Simon has taken this seriously enough to alert the authorities. Let's see what the others are up to. I've already spoken to Ross; he's off to talk to the drone systems people. I'll just let him know about the mesh."

She quickly sent a message to Ross: 'Hope you're not still feeling blue.' It bounced back.

"Hmm, that's odd. His screen's switched off. I'll worry about that later. Let's try the others."

Three times she sent, 'How's your Sunday going? Isn't this blue sky incredible?'

She sat back down on the bench and took a bite from a small piece of quiche, waiting for a response.

Joel's came first. 'Coffee with Ross. He's droning on as usual.'

"Hah, brilliant, so Ross has pulled Joel in to help him. Good thinking."

Noor's reply beeped. 'Pretty quiet. How's Franklin?'

Cameron thought for a moment and sent a reply. 'Had to see a specialist. Not sure about the root of the problem. I'll speak to you soon.' She crossed her fingers that Noor could work through the tortuous phrasing and understand what was happening.

Pete hadn't responded. "He's probably out diving. He'll be in touch when he surfaces." She picked up her wine glass and looked at Andy. "Anything else going on that I should know about?"

"Maybe. There are some reports coming through from the US about rogue security bots on the rampage. Some shootings. Reports possible fatalities."

"Oh no, that's awful." Sameena looked horrified. "Is it widespread? I have family in Texas."

Andy nodded, sombre. "Yes, nothing breaking on the news channels just yet. We're verifying sources, but at least twelve states appear to be involved."

"I need to get on the forums. Give me a minute."

Cameron chose to use her private connection in the attic, bounding back up the stairs again. She set the location to a town in California, and logged on. Sure enough, there was chaos.

"SimCavalier, glad you're here."

"What are we up to so far, Storm Franklin?"

"You think this is part of the pattern? In that case it's Galileo," typed Cameron. "I'm so sorry to see this, guys, it's dreadful."

"Sunday morning. Lots of people out and about, kids going to sports clubs, folk going to church. Just awful."

"Do you need help with a fix?"

"No. We're good, thanks, SimCavalier. Uploaded it already, and it seems to be stopping them in their tracks."

"Anyone isolated the cause?"

"Well, we're not sure. A bunch of us rolled out security updates on the robocops last week. Thought they were tight. Guess we were wrong."

Cameron sighed. "Same thing we're seeing. There's a chance of a compromise at update level. Get into the source servers, see what you can find."

"Really? That's mad."

"How far ahead was this planned, anyway?"

"What the hell are we dealing with?"

"No idea, guys, just know that it's everywhere. Listen, I'm going to try something here. We may need tighter security. Keep your Bluetooth devices to hand. Stay safe. Be vigilant."

Cameron went to sign off the group, then hesitated.

What was going on with the crypto futures thread? She navigated over to it. There was a buzz around the topic. After weeks of dismissing the ideas Ross had posted, a few analysts were reporting similar trends. Good to see others picking up on it independently. They might still have a chance to minimise profiteering from this wave of attacks. She dropped a post onto the thread.

"Can the cryptocurrency be destabilised quickly?"

Responses came back swiftly.

"Denial of Service attacks on banking systems?"

"Yes, a run on currency when the banks came back online would do it. Wouldn't a DDoS stop them from realising their trades, though? Any more?"

"Power outages, same effect?"

"Security fork adoption conflicts?"

"The community would have to pretty badly divided to stop a genuine security fork being applied. We're all friends here, aren't we?"

There was a chorus of virtual assent and amused chatter.

"Anything that takes away people's trust in machines, SimCavalier. Power outages, sure, but trust is eroding already."

"Fair point. Robocops, drones, credentialing… The disturbances have all helped to raise the crypto value against hard currency, but there may be a tipping point."

"We're looking out for development, SimCavalier."

"Thanks guys. Stay safe."

She logged off and sat staring at the blank screen.

Ben came upstairs to find her deep in thought. "You okay? What's the news from America?"

"It's grim. Rogue robocops. Same story, the updates were applied and malicious code has been dropped in at the same time. I think there will be a lot of fatalities. They've managed to close them down, thank goodness." She sighed, reflecting on the horror of this latest attack.

"What now?"

Cameron shook herself. "I think we're reaching a peak. The things that have happened over the past few hours or so have gone beyond causing unrest. Now they're challenging our reliance on machines. They're ready to take their profits." She looked up at her boyfriend. "Ben, you know what you were saying about data sensors in components? Let me get on with building this mesh, and then we need to talk to Charlie."

She took a deep breath and started typing. The virus she was creating would spread from one Bluetooth device to the next, harnessing speakers and headsets, signage and adverts, building an alternative internet. Their communications would be hidden from view.

Gradually, the mesh network took shape.

•

Pete and his friends clambered off the dive boat, lugging their gear onto the pier. They gave the skipper a cheery wave as he cast off and headed for his berth.

"Great dive." The GPS had not betrayed them this

time. The skipper had put them straight over the wreck they'd been looking for, in perfect conditions.

Pete unzipped his buddy's dry suit and turned so his friend could do the same. He felt the top of his head gingerly. "I think I caught the sun out there."

There was a gale of laughter.

"That'll teach you," said one of the other divers sternly. "I offered you sunblock, but no. Honestly, men." She grinned.

The group gradually stripped off their layers and changed into shorts and t-shirts. Their gear was carefully stowed in bags and boxes, and Pete summoned an autotrailer to carry the heavy load back along the harbour.

"Who's coming for a pint?" asked his buddy, as they followed the trailer to the car park.

"Not me, sorry," replied Pete. "I have to get back." He hailed an autocar and transferred his kit into it. "See you all next week. Train station, please." The little car's motor strained as it carted the heavy equipment up a short hill, settling as it reached the main road. They trundled towards the main line station; there was a train to London due in a few minutes. Perfect timing.

As they approached the station car park, the vehicle ground to a halt. The doors popped open and Pete started with surprise. "Oh. Autocar swarm." He jumped out and grabbed his gear before the little car swept off to join its fellows on a recharging mercy mission. The platform was only a short walk away; he wouldn't miss the train.

Settling into his seat, bags carefully stowed, Pete finally

switched on his smartscreen. A message popped straight up for his attention. 'How's your Sunday going? Isn't this blue sky incredible?'

He was immediately on alert – and impressed. There must be something serious going down if Cameron had acted on the emergency plan they'd put together years ago. He scanned the news channels. Reports of rogue robocops in America. Nothing more on the drone crashes. What was happening under the radar? Ah, the last item on the bulletin, a scheduled maintenance warning for Bluetooth. Clever girl.

Pete sent a quick reply: 'Nice dive. Swarming all over the wreck. Some pretty blue fish down there too.' He switched off his smartscreen and went to his bag. In an inside pocket, rarely used but always charged, lay his Bluetooth headset. He sat back down in his seat and waited patiently for the call, looking out of the window.

The train was rattling on towards London. Fast run this afternoon, he thought. It looked as if the train wasn't stopping at its usual stations. They passed through one, and he caught glimpses of a crowded platform, and shocked faces as people jumped backwards. That wasn't right.

A mutter of concern and disbelief rose in the carriage. Pete looked around, then stood up and started to walk towards the front of the train. He could see the track curving away ahead of them, and another station just visible in the distance. They passed green signals at speed, some of the old lights still operating despite the automated carriages that had been running for years. To his horror, Pete saw another train at the station, and realised they were on the same tracks.

He threw himself into a seat, bellowing "we're going to crash," at the top of his voice. He put his feet flat on the floor, pressed his head and body against the high seat back, and clutched the armrests. The impact came, and he fell into blackness.

•

Cameron's screen beeped just as Ben appeared to check on her progress. "I was right, Pete was diving. Hmm, he says there's been a car swarm. Probably a local outage. Hope so."

She replied quickly. 'Sounds great. Hope you're doing some research.'

"There we go. He'll come back with details on that swarm for us. Probably nothing to worry about."

"How's it going?" asked Ben.

"Done. It'll take a little while to spread. Let's go downstairs."

Returning to the shady garden and flopping back in her seat, Cameron turned to Charlie. "Ben was telling me about sensors that are built into components." She glanced at Ben. "You can explain it better than me."

"Uh, okay. I produce designs for 3D printing. We've got some up on the Mars mission. Anyway, some of these include sensor elements that send feedback to our systems so we can refine the design, materials mix, and so on."

Charlie nodded. "I know the type of thing. Yes, a lot of our larger components have feedback loops in. All the prototype stuff too. Valuable data. We don't collect ourselves, of course. We just produce the physical items." He looked at Cameron. "Why?"

"Ben tells me there's been a hiatus in data capture. Nothing arriving at the servers, but the network is showing no errors. Can you check with your designers that their data is arriving cleanly? I'm hoping it's just a local problem."

"Sure," replied Charlie, "but what do design sensors have to do with your line of work?"

"Not sure yet. Just a feeling I have. Charlie, Ben, how much processing power would an average component sensor have? How many components are we talking about? And can you control them?"

"They're very small, but quite powerful for their size, I guess… and millions, maybe billions of them in circulation. As for control… yeah, there is a way to interrogate them, refine the data capture in an existing sensor."

"Oh, that's great," said Cameron, her voice dripping with sarcasm. "An old-school Mirai botnet ready to roll."

Ben and Charlie looked at her blankly.

"What's a Mirai…?" asked Ben.

"Botnet. It's a clever little trick. We've been looking for something like this. It's one of the most likely attack scenarios. A botnet can harness the processing power of a huge network of devices and flood a site with traffic."

She looked at Charlie soberly. "I'm sorry, I really can't stay. I have to get back. This is going haywire." She stood up. "I'll order a taxi."

Cameron walked into the house and turned to the nearest screen. The news channel was running.

"Breaking: train services across the UK have been suspended pending urgent investigations, following a serious crash between a stationary carriage waiting at a platform, and an out of control train which had jumped several stop points at high speed." Images of twisted metal and a damaged station frontage showed on the screen, human and robot paramedics attending to casualties.

Cameron swore.

"We're going to have to get an auto car all the way back to London. Trains are off."

"Cars are off too," said Charlie, following her in. "There was a report earlier of a swarm; all cars out of action."

"Dammit, that'll be the swarm Pete saw. I hoped it was local. I guess it wasn't. Looks like I'm stranded."

"There are worse places," reminded her brother. "And you can work from here. Let me know if there's anything you need. Think about it, if this carries on, I'm stranded too. I'm not fit enough to cycle to work tomorrow, and there's probably no point if none of the staff can get in either."

Cameron couldn't help giggling at the thought of her brother on his bike. "It'd do you good. Right, I'm going

to finish off that mesh network. Send coffee and snacks."
She climbed back up to her attic, and set to work.

•

At the bank, Ella, Susie, and Sandeep were trawling through the latest updates they'd made to the systems, looking for any clue to compromises, any hint of malicious code. Sir Simon and Bill were watching the crypto futures market like a hawk, jumping at any blip.

"Trading's slowed right down. We must be close to the peak."

"How's the value looking?"

"Still artificially high. It's got to drop. This is like the thick air before a storm hits. Any moment now, we're going to get drenched. Well, metaphorically speaking," added Bill, as Sir Simon looked sidelong at him.

Ella's screen pinged.

'All set,' it said, followed by a link.

"Oh, good girl. Okay, we have open comms with Cameron."

They all donned their headsets.

"Afternoon, everyone. Hi Ella, you have Susie and Sandeep with you?"

The other two said hello.

"Noor, you at home?"

"No, Cameron, I'm in the office. I thought I'd be more useful here."

"Good thinking. Joel, you have Ross?"

"No, he headed off an hour ago. Said he had some things to sort out. Haven't you heard from him?"

"Not a word since we spoke earlier. He hasn't replied to any messages either." Odd, she thought. What had he wanted to tell her this morning?

"Where's Pete?" asked Ella.

"He's been diving. He'll be on his way back from the coast. Probably stuck waiting for a train. I'm sure he'll join us as soon as he can."

Bill sat in the background, grinning. He loved watching this team work. They were a great unit.

"Let's roll," said Cameron. "First off, it looks like there is a Mirai botnet taking shape out there. It won't be a coincidence. We all need to be vigilant for a DDoS attack."

"Is that the attack you anticipate will cause a drop in cryptocurrency values?" asked Sir Simon.

"Possibly," answered Ella. "Although it could mask something else. It's a tough attack to defend against. But something doesn't quite fit. If they block the servers, they won't be able to complete their trades. Something else has to give first. I think they'll take their profits, and then use a DDoS attack to mask their escape."

"No unusual traffic reported, Cameron, but we'll keep our eyes peeled," replied Sandeep.

"What have we got so far? Joel – drones? Anything?"

"Yeah. There's a nasty bit of code attached to one of the recent update files. Ross and I cobbled together a patch and that's on its way out now."

"Nice one. Fast work. Can you transmit copy?"

"Sure." There was a pause. "There you go. Cameron, something odd though. I checked out the work that the guys in the US have been doing on the rogue robocops. There are a lot of similarities with the patch, but I haven't seen the code they found yet."

Cameron was taken aback. "You're saying it's the same attack?"

"It's not impossible. The first reports came in very early this morning, US time. Around the same time as the drones went haywire."

Noor broke in to the conversation. "You know this train crash? There were reports of service glitches all over the place from around the same time. Coincidence?"

"Hmm, maybe not. What else has happened today?"

"Autocar swarm?"

"That was later. That started this afternoon."

"Yes… but it's still going, and it's country-wide. What are they swarming to fix?"

They were all silent for a moment, before the horrifying truth swept over them.

"Power distribution. The power distributors are down. Forget bots and drones and trains… this is it. This is where the country loses confidence in tech."

There was a shout from Bill. "It's dropping."

They watched as the value of cryptocurrency went into freefall, before the lights flickered and went out.

12: BLACKOUT

Ella gave a startled cry as the lights went out. "What happened?"

"Power's gone," replied Bill. "The priority for the bank's emergency power generation is keeping those servers running, nothing else. Is your network still running?"

"Yes, no problem. These are very low power devices, and won't need charging for a while." Ella did a quick rollcall.

"Noor here. I'm fine here in the office. The solar panels are at top production, and the batteries are full."

"I'm still here," Joel called, "but I don't have batteries. All our excess generation goes straight to the grid, and we're purely solar too. I won't have power after nightfall."

"I think we're alright. Roof full of panels and batteries in the cellar," replied Cameron. "But that's autocars and trains out of action. No one can go anywhere."

"What do we do now?" asked Noor. "If this was a call from a client, what would we be doing?"

"We'd be heading to their site ready to quarantine, fix and patch," replied Joel, "or we'd be straight on the net advising their people what to do. We can't do either right now."

Cameron paused as a thought struck her. "Actually, we can. I bet I can get there. And I think it'll be fun."

•

Deep in the bank, Ella and Susie looked at each other in the dim light that streamed in from the ground level skylights. They held their breath, and to their relief heard the gentle whirr of the servers, still running.

"Emergency power saving," explained Sir Simon. "We have full batteries which keep the servers and security systems online in the event of an outage. The roof panels will keep the batteries topped up."

"You can keep working, but we don't have any additional comms," explained Bill.

"Let's get cracking, then," said Sandeep. "You captured Joel's fix, didn't you, Ella? If he's right, then the same worm has infected all systems. That'll help us find any compromise here and fix it."

"Brilliant, Sandeep. Good thinking."

"What about the scenarios we ran? We know the cryptocurrency price has started falling. We can't see how far this spreads, or if they've started taking profits, but we can be ready for when the power comes back."

"What do you mean, Ms Stanford?"

"Well, Sir Simon, this attack should send clear signals around your industry that there really is something wrong. You've laid the foundations, your voice is one they listen to, and you got the Prime Minister to support you. I'd be surprised if trading hasn't been suspended already."

Bill nodded. "But what do we have to prepare for?" he asked.

"Cameron says there was a botnet out there. A DDoS attack would tie the systems up, and could mask other things. These people may have robbed the bank, but they haven't made it out of the door yet."

Realisation dawned.

"If we're ready for them, we can block the exits? Is that what you're saying?"

Ella nodded. "Let's get to work."

•

Ross cycled steadily south through the London suburbs towards the Thames from Joel's home. He had no real idea where to go. The roads were deserted, quieter than a normal Sunday. A few drones were flying; the fix he and Joel had delivered had been tested and deployed. He found himself heading for the small city airport. For a moment it crossed his mind to jump on a plane, leave the country, hide himself. But no. Passing through the border would flag his location straight up to anyone who was watching – and he had no doubt that someone was.

He reached the river. Was this the end of the road? As he stared into the sluggish current, he caught sight of an old Victorian brick building, perfectly round, incongruous in its modern setting: the Woolwich foot tunnel.

Ross pulled himself from the brink, and wheeled his bike towards the entrance and down the old stairs. The tunnel was dingy, lights flickering, water dripping. He cycled where he could, and trudged the rest of the half-kilometre down under the Thames and up to the south bank. As he reached the end, the lights behind him were suddenly extinguished. He shivered. He didn't know what had caused it, but he was glad to be out in the sunlight.

Cycling onwards, he passed a cluster of local shops, and realised he was hungry. He propped his bike against a wall, and approached the door of a general store, hesitating when he saw that although the door was open, the lights were off.

"You open?" he called.

"Yeah, mate, but we got no power. About to shut up shop."

Ross stepped in to the gloom. "Just wanted a sandwich? Any food left?"

The shopkeeper shrugged. "All the fresh stuff'll have to be chucked if the power don't come back. Help yourself. Can't take your money anyways." He ambled over towards Ross, scowling. "Should've bought into that solar network when I had the chance."

"This has got to be the first blanket outage since… oh… 2034?" said Ross, as he picked up some cold meat, cheese and bread. "Remember that? I was still at school, just. Took a few hours to fix. Chaos."

"World's gone crazy today, innit. Drones, trains, and

what about America, eh? Thought they'd seen the last of their mass shootings, and then the 'bots get them."

Ross muttered in agreement, thanked the shopkeeper, and took his leave. A plan was starting to form in his head. The problem had to be at the distribution centres. There was enough power being generated, he reflected, as the sun beat down, a light breeze blew, and the river flowed. SussexGrid was one of their clients. Maybe he had a chance to redeem himself. Could he make it there before dark? He retrieved his bike, and turned away from the river, heading south with renewed purpose.

•

Cameron's eyes were dancing as she explained her plan to Charlie, Sameena, Ben and Andy.

"…if I get to the plant, I think the fix we already have will solve the problem. Where did Aunt Vicky stow it?"

"It's at the back of one of the barns on Jack's farm down the village," said Charlie.

"You'd better ask your aunt before you borrow it," joked Andy. "And be home before midnight."

Ben laughed.

"But Cameron," said Sameena, worriedly, "you can't drive."

"That's okay," replied Cameron. She grinned at Ben. "I know a man who can."

Andy, Cameron and Ben trooped up the hill. Donald was lounging on the path in front of Aunt Vicky's door, a mound of ginger fur. Jasper growled at him. Donald took no notice. Boris the tabby was sitting on Andy's doorstep, not taking his eyes from his rival.

"Bit of a fight, I reckon," sighed Andy. "Boris keeps trying to take back control but Donald rides roughshod over him. Cats. Honestly." He skirted around the lurking felines and called into the back garden. "Vicky? Are you home?"

An indistinct reply came, and the three of them crowded round the side of the house to find Aunt Vicky calmly tidying her flowerbeds. She stood up, brushing down her skirt.

"Hello Andy. Oh, Cameron, darling, and Ben. How lovely. I'd offer you a cup of tea but I can't get anything to work. What can I do for you?"

Cameron glanced at Ben. "Um, Aunt Vicky, can I borrow your car?"

She had never before seen her aunt lost for words.

"Oh, really?" she finally stammered. "But… It's been covered in hay for years. It will need a wash. And I don't even know if it will work."

Cameron laughed. "Oh, Aunt Vicky. I'm sure it'll be fine." She crossed her fingers behind her back. "So, do you have a key?"

"Yes, dear." She pulled herself together. "But do you have a driver? I'm sure I can remember…"

"It's fine," interjected Ben. "I can drive. My dad was a real petrolhead. I haven't done it for a few years, but I know what I'm doing." Aunt Vicky looked relieved.

Scurrying into the dark interior of the house, she scuffled around in a drawer, and finally extracted a key fob.

"I don't think there'll be any charge in the battery, but the car isn't locked. You know where it is?"

Cameron nodded, and threw her arms round her aunt. "Thank you so much." She and Ben dashed back out of the garden, and made their way up the village street to the farm.

Jack showed them to the barn, which lay at the top of a long track that sloped down towards the road. "It's that yellow one, at the back. This one here's mine. That one belongs to the lad at the pub…"

Ben stared. "You have quite a collection."

"Aye, it seemed a shame to scrap them. Good memories."

"Can we get hold of any fuel?" Jack frowned.

"I'm not so sure. There used to be a service station up at the junction, but I don't think there's much left in the tanks under that concrete. How far do you need to go?"

"At least two hundred kilometres, possibly more."

Jack shook his head. "There's your problem. You won't have the range."

Ben was thinking hard. "What did all these run on?"

"Well, that yellow car of your aunt's was petrol. Nippy little thing. She used to frighten the life out of me, and my stock, bombing round the lanes. My old pickup truck's diesel, all the farm vehicles were until we switched to electric. Don't know about the other ones."

"Cameron, how far away is Mandisa? She's a scientist,

isn't she? Could she get hold of enough ethanol to fill a tank?"

"She lives right on the other side of the town, and her lab is further away again. Is there anything else we could use? Something we'd be able to make here?"

"Not for a petrol engine," Ben shook his head. "But diesel, now… Jack, could we use your pickup, instead?"

Jack nodded. "Certainly. I'll get the key." He turned away towards the house. Cameron looked puzzled.

"Why does that make a difference?"

Ben laughed. "Totally different engines. The truck will run on vegetable oil. There's no shortage of that."

Jack came back and proffered and old key at Ben. "There you go, son. All yours. Let's get her running. There's enough fuel left in there to get you a few miles, charge up the battery. I sneak her out for a spin from time to time, but not enough to keep a charge. That's why she's parked on top of a hill. Have you done this before?" Ben shook his head. "Right, you push."

The farmer clambered into the cab and turned the key. There was a click, but nothing more. "Dead as a dodo. Now, if this happens again, put her in second gear and roll her. Try and hold the clutch right at the biting point. It'll catch. Now, push."

Ben and Cameron pushed the truck laboriously out of the barn. As it hit the gradient, it gathered its own momentum. They stood and watched as it rolled down the hill, and cheered when the engine coughed into life, a cloud of smoke bursting from the exhaust. Jack drove onto the main road and out of sight. He returned a few minutes later, pulling up at the gate, the engine idling.

"Right, son, hop in. She's all yours. Take care to park at the top of a hill. Bring her back in one piece."

Stammering out their thanks, Ben took Jack's place at the wheel, and Cameron climbed up beside him in the passenger seat. Ben drove cautiously along the street to Charlie's house.

"I'll wait here. We're at the bottom of a hill. Get some oil. And a map. Do you know where we're going?"

Cameron jumped out and ran around to the garden. "We're sorted. Come and look. We've got Jack's old pickup working."

The whole family rushed to the road, the children distracted from playing.

"Ewww, it smells," complained Tara, pinching her nose.

"Cool," said Dilan, impressed.

Nina took several photographs with her screen, recording the pickup from all angles and Ben grinning in the driver's seat.

Cameron drew her sister-in-law aside. "Sameena, I need as many bottles or cans of vegetable oil as you can find. And some water would be good too. I'm just going to get a map." She rushed upstairs, and brought a map up on the computer screen. Transferring it to her smartscreen, she checked it could be viewed offline. All good. She did the same with the fix file that Joel had sent.

An idea occurred to her; she made a quick call. "Joel, you live just off the M25, don't you? We have transport.

We'll collect you in an hour. We're going to SussexGrid. I'll call you when we get close for directions."

"That's great, Cameron. Nice one," replied Joel. "I'll see you shortly."

Turning her attention to Noor, she thought through her plans. "Keep trying to get hold of Pete. I lost contact with him. Could be a faulty Bluetooth device."

Noor nodded. "I hope so, Cameron."

"Get onto the forums and see who is still live, try and get some direct connections established, and find out what's happening globally. Get Joel's drone fix out as far as possible and see if it works for other reported failures. I bet it will. If you can, start a movement to suspend cryptocurrency trading, and warn people to watch out for a DDoS attack. I'm sure that's the next step, something to help them get their money out."

"Okay, Cameron, I'm on it. Good luck."

Cameron rushed back downstairs. Sameena had loaded several bottles of water and a bag with cake and sandwiches into the truck, along with couple of cans of vegetable oil. Ben was cautiously filling the tank with a third. He looked up. "Ready?"

"Ready." She jumped into the cab and pulled on her sunglasses. "Ready as I'll ever be."

•

Sir Simon Winchester was frustrated. Isolated in the bank, the tech experts were working hard to prepare for the next storm. That might protect his small part of the financial world, but it would not be enough to stop this threat in the shadows. It had to be a team effort.

He reflected on the skilful planning that had gone into this unprecedented series of attacks. First, destabilise hard currency through unrest. Next, unleash a worm to flip the market, destroying confidence in tech. That must have been a long time in the making, he realised, to penetrate so completely, and to execute simultaneously. The power outage triggered by the same worm isolates the decision makers, keeps trades running long enough to realise a handsome profit. Then, if Cameron's team were right, another wave to ensure the perpetrators made good their escape. Extraordinary. Unprecedented.

How could he spread the word?

"Ms Stanford?"

Ella looked up, startled.

"Your offices are nearby, are they not?"

"About twenty minutes' walk, yes."

"I presume that you have a number of communication channels that you can access from those offices? Power, too? I would expect no less."

Ella nodded. "Yes. It's well set up."

"What if I were to go in person to your offices and attempt to contact my counterparts in the industry? That may be a step towards minimising the damage from this market manipulation."

Sandeep blinked. "What a great idea. We're very close to completing this fix, it's taken no time thanks to Joel's input. Do we really need to stay down here, Ella? Can we run the possible attack scenarios from the office?"

"Can't see why not. Susie, why don't you go over with Sir Simon. Sandeep, Bill and I can stay here. When the power comes back, we'll need to be ready to fight."

Susie gratefully grabbed her bag and flashed a grin at Ella. "It'll be good to get out in the fresh air. I'll call you when we get there." She positively scampered out of the door, followed by Sir Simon.

They walked down to London Bridge. There were no cars on the streets. They were all still attached to their swarm hosts, feeding in every Joule they could generate in a fruitless attempt to keep the city's infrastructure running. Bicycles whizzed freely over the bridge, and a river ferry, running under its own solar power, hooted mournfully. The city still functioned, after a fashion.

Wind turbines all up the Thames were whirring gently as a light breeze blew, but the power they generated remained untapped. Passing the market, quiet on a lazy Sunday afternoon, they turned into a side street and arrived at the door of Argentum Associates. Susie presented her credentials and the door slid open: no problem with the power or the network here. Climbing the stairs, Susie and Sir Simon entered the office, to find Noor busy on a monitor, a Bluetooth speaker on the table beside her, and a cup of hot coffee in her hand.

"Hi Susie. Oh – hello, Sir Simon."

"Ah, coffee, what a great idea. The only things on at

the bank are the servers and the security systems. Coffee machines are non-essential."

Susie slipped a mug into place. "Cappuccino."

Sir Simon smiled. "You're right, Ms Lu. I must review those protocols. Good evening, Ms Khawaja. I'll have a double espresso, please."

Susie gave Noor a quick status update. "Ella and Sandeep have almost finished cleaning the systems and they're standing by for the next challenge. How are you getting on here?"

"I still can't raise Pete, and Ross has simply disappeared. But Cameron – oh my word – she and Ben have managed to get an old car running, and they're on their way to SussexGrid. They've just picked up Joel. It's brilliant."

"How marvellous," said Sir Simon. "She's a very resourceful woman, isn't she?"

"I'm in touch with as many teams as I can find," continued Noor. "There are a lot of people offline, but those of us that are able are working towards fixing the outage worldwide."

"This is the reason I've joined you here," explained Sir Simon. "If you can help me to connect with fellow decision makers in the currency markets, I hope we can come to an agreement to suspend trading as soon as the power is restored. That would limit the profits for this group, whoever they are, to the money they have already made. If thereafter they are prevented from withdrawing those funds, so much the better. However, we must take steps to mitigate our losses immediately."

Noor understood perfectly. "Take this monitor." She indicated a blank screen, which glowed into life at her touch. "Susie, can you keep an eye on the forums. Let's get to work."

•

The ancient pickup truck pulled, wheezing, into the car park at SussexGrid. Ben looked around frantically for a good place to park, and spotted a service road sloping down behind the offices that fronted the distribution plant.

"That'll do." He stopped the truck at the top of the slope, ready to roll if its battery died. "I'm going to give this engine a bit of TLC. You go and save the world." He gave Cameron a kiss as she shouldered her bag and headed for the door.

Joel reached out and shook Ben's hand. "Awesome drive, man. Reminded me of being back in the army. Nice work." He grinned, and followed his boss towards the offices.

The door opened, and a startled security guard let them in. The company's chief technology officer came running to the foyer. "Cameron! We weren't expecting you, but you are a sight for sore eyes. Have you fixed it already?"

Cameron laughed. "Nice to see you too, Julia. I love your confidence. It's actually possible that we have fixed it. Let's see what we're dealing with."

Cameron and Joel followed her to the nerve centre of the installation, and started work.

A short time later, the security guard opened the door again to a dishevelled-looking young man with ginger hair. "Your colleagues have already arrived. You know where you're going. Let me take care of your bike."

•

Stranded by his swarming autocar, the stranger had given up on Ross returning to his home. In frustration, he prowled around the outside of the house, and found a window ajar. After several attempts, he managed to force it fully open. It was a struggle to get through, especially without alerting any neighbours, although the overgrown trees in the garden shielded his efforts from most casual gazes. Must lose some weight, he muttered to himself.

Inside, he started to search, room by room, for any clues to the disappearance of his prey. On a table he found two screens, abandoned and switched off. One he managed to open: the only data on it showed communication with the hub, and with the stranger himself. The other was impenetrably sealed with biometric markers. He threw it to the floor in disgust.

As he walked back along the hall towards the bedroom where he had entered, the daylight cast a shadow around a regular tear in the wallpaper. Pausing, he ripped at the flap. The tear had been made deliberately, and recently.

What had been hidden under there? He tore the paper off and dug with his fingers into the hole in the wall, past the obsolete control panel, feeling his way.

At SussexGrid, Julia triumphantly flipped a switch, and there was a rush of glorious light. A ragged cheer went up from the assembled team.

The stranger felt an overwhelming sharp pain travel from his hand into his body. There was bang, and he fell backwards to the carpet. He did not move.

•

"The power's back on," cried Ella as the lights flicked back on and screens lit up.

In the office, Susie and Sir Simon jumped at the sound of Ella's voice emanating from the speaker.

"Bill, get up to the boardroom, check the market feeds," Sir Simon's voice sounded over the speaker in the operations room. "I think we've managed to close it down."

Bill rushed out of the room.

Ella turned to Sandeep. "Right, I guess we'd better brace ourselves. Keep an eye on the traffic."

Sure enough, as they watched, the traffic to the bank's servers started rising steadily.

"I can't believe it's started so quickly," said Sandeep.

"It makes sense," replied Ella. "If they really have managed to stop trading, then whoever is behind this knows we've rumbled them. They'll be trying to get their profits out now. Noor, did you catch that? We believe the DDoS attack has been initiated."

"Confirming that," replied Noor. "Reports coming in from all over the place. At least we were all ready. What do you think it's masking?"

Bill came flying back through the door. "Futures trading on cryptocurrency markets is suspended, but there's something else going on. Alerts on all the client accounts. Balances are yoyoing up and down. There are transfers happening, but we can't tell where they're going to."

"That's it!" yelled Ella. "They're taking the scenic route through other people's accounts. Noor, check whether this pattern is holding elsewhere. We've closed down all the vulnerabilities in the servers, but they're obfuscating the real transactions. Covering their tracks. I think it's just a smokescreen."

Noor was frantically keeping track of all the forum activity. "That hot team on the east coast have picked up on it. They're working on it."

"I'm tracking the paths… there's a clear line emerging towards a set of wallets. Noor, transmit these wallet addresses… see what people come up with."

There was a shout of triumph across the office. "East Coast confirmed, one of the wallet addresses matches Speakeasy."

"Unbelievable," cried Ella. "Why would they do that?"

"Showing off? Reminding us all who started this? It's pretty much empty. I think that's their signature flourish."

"DDoS has slowed. Traffic falling back to normal levels," reported Sandeep.

Ella sagged in her chair. "They took their money, then. We failed in the end."

Sir Simon's voice was strong and positive. "No, Ms Stanford, you did not fail. The amounts they got away with were tiny compared to the possible profits. They haven't had the payoff they'd expect from all this effort. You should be proud of yourselves. All of you."

•

In the critical care ward of Southern Infirmary, Dr Roberts perked up as the main lighting flickered back on. Her patient was breathing quietly, monitors steady, condition stable.

"Do we have any ID yet?" she asked her colleague.

"Possibly," he responded. "When he was brought in, he only had the clothes on his back and a Bluetooth headset. Transport police have found an unclaimed set of bags further back in the train." He looked round as the curtain twitched and a uniformed newcomer entered the cubicle.

"Can we try this smartscreen, doctor?"

Dr Roberts nodded. She picked up the patient's limp hand and pressed his thumb to the screen. It lit up instantly.

"Brilliant. And a lot of messages waiting. Someone is missing this lad."

The policeman smiled. "I'll go and give them the good news, shall I?"

"Yes please." The doctor turned as her patient stirred. "Hello, Pete. How are you feeling? I'm Dr Roberts. You've been involved in a train crash. Everything is going to be just fine."

•

The pickup truck trundled along the motorway. Ross's bike lay in the back, and Joel, Cameron and Ross were crammed together in the cab while Ben drove steadily home. The power restored, cars were moving on the road again. Very few had passengers. Most were empty, returning from their swarm hosts to their usual charging points, job done. Those people who were travelling looked up in amazement as the battered old vehicle made its stately way along the carriageway.

Joel jumped out at his home, and Ross clambered out too and hauled his bike over the tailgate. "I'm going to crash in Joel's spare room tonight. Thanks, Ben. And thank you, Cameron." He paused. "Cameron… I need to tell you something." He hung his head. "The tipoff to the news channels. I'm so sorry. It was me."

He was close to tears.

Stunned, Cameron jumped out of the cab and hugged him awkwardly. "I had no idea, Ross. Don't worry. No harm done in the end. Let's talk properly tomorrow."

Ross nodded. There was going to be a lot to cover.

"We'd better get going," warned Ben. "I don't trust these headlights." He coaxed the idling engine into life. Cameron took her place at his side again and they continued on their way.

The lights were still on at Charlie's house as the truck pulled up at the gate. Cameron clambered down from the cab as her brother emerged from the front door, alerted by the throaty growl of the engine.

"I don't believe it. You made it."

Andy was close behind him. "Cameron, I swear, I would give anything to run that story. You bloody marvel."

Cameron grinned at him. "It is quite a story, isn't it? And it deserves to be told, if only to warn people what could happen, what is likely to happen again. I'll give you your scoop, but I stay in the shadows."

The truck horn beeped behind her.

"We'd better get this beauty back to Jack. He'll want to know we've taken care of her." Taking her seat in the cab for the last time, Cameron waved. "Andy, we'll talk tomorrow. Charlie, we'll be back in a jiffy."

•

Monday morning dawned, unseasonably cold and drizzly. Cameron curled up tight against Ben's back, ignoring the light that had disturbed her sleep.

Ben, too, was stirring. "Ohh, I am aching all over. Driving hurts. My shoulders. My back." He stretched, and Cameron protested.

"If you're going to kick me out of bed, I may as well go and get some coffee."

She grabbed the red bathrobe and padded down the stairs, heading for the kitchen, where she found Charlie already up and watching the news channels.

"All credit for the fast resolution of these unprecedented attacks must go to the talented teams of threat intelligence operatives with whom it has been my pleasure to work," said Sir Simon to the interviewer.

"Can you give us details of the agency the bank has worked with, Sir Simon?"

"I'm sorry, I can't identify them. It's best if they remain anonymous; their role at the forefront of the war against cyber crime is extremely sensitive."

Cameron smiled. "Andy will get his story, no problem. I may have to reconsider our blanket secrecy. It might be better to be a little open. It may even give us more protection and help in the long term."

The kettle boiled, and Charlie filled four mugs with strong coffee.

"Are you staying another day?"

"No," Cameron sighed. "There's a lot of clearing up to do. Everyone's in the office this morning. I should go and visit Pete in hospital. The cat will be going loopy and she'll need feeding. And Ben has to get back to work."

Charlie took a good look at his little sister. "He's a keeper, Cam. You know that, don't you?"

She nodded. "Yes, Charlie. I know."

ACKNOWLEDGEMENTS

This book would not have been written without months of persuasion from David Morton of itsw.co (http://itsw.co/), who eventually convinced me to put the first five hundred words down on paper. Lorraine Ellison's howls of laughter at an early snippet of the adventures of Donald the Cat finally pushed me to write the rest. Further thanks to David for curbing the wilder improbable tech scenarios that tumbled from my imagination chapter by chapter, to Rosie Brent and Vicky Burke who each read the first complete draft, enjoyed it, and suggested some key changes, and to my remarkably patient family. Most of the tech in this book already exists in some form or another, and I'm looking forward to seeing how our lives change over the next few decades.

•

Find out more about the author at katebaucherel.com

Printed in Great Britain
by Amazon